David Beers

The Devil's Dream: A Nightmare

This book was professionally typeset on Reedsy.
Find out more at reedsy.com

Contents

One 1

Two 9

Three 11

Four 22

Five 33

Six 43

Seven 47

Eight 61

Nine 70

Ten 82

Eleven 97

Twelve 106

Thirteen 119

Fourteen 131

Fifteen 150

Sixteen 160

Seventeen 171

Eighteen 175

Nineteen 185

Twenty 201

On Purpose and Other Things 204

The Devil's Dream: Part III 205

Also by David Beers 213

1

One

Allison Moore watched her daughter descend the steps. Marley walked slow, taking each step as if she wasn't completely sure it would be there when her foot arrived. Allison stood, smiling, in no hurry to do anything else. Marley took these same steps every day and she took them at the same speed. The world had made Allison move at a different speed for so long, and now she had adapted to the pace Marley needed. The world and its callings no longer mattered, not outside of making sure that Marley had food and a roof.

Allison had the food ready this morning, sitting on the kitchen table. It took Marley five minutes to walk anywhere in the house, so Allison never poured the milk into the cereal before Marley sat. She would do it once Marley was in place and ready to eat.

She had to make sure Marley was at the table an hour and a half before the bus arrived to pick her up. Things moved slow around Allison's house, and that was okay. It was better than okay, really, because she had her daughter at home, as opposed to the glorified psychiatric ward she had resided in for two years. Those years had been tough. Spending as much time as possible at the ward, only leaving at bedtime each day and only then because her little girl needed routine.

That's what Allison wanted now for her daughter: routine. She didn't want anything out of the ordinary to appear, didn't want to surprise Marley at all. Marley needed order and that meant Allison's life contained it too. After breakfast, Marley would head back upstairs and dress. Allison originally thought that it would be easier if they dressed Marley and then brought her down to eat, that way things would move quicker. Marley didn't like doing it that way, though. She actually had refused, and Allison smiled when she did. Marley rarely, if ever, took an interest in anything and for her to demonstrate that she didn't want to dress first, that she would rather eat breakfast in her pajamas--well that was a miracle for Allison. So every morning Allison brought Marley down, took her back up, and then Allison would walk her to the bus stop where they waited together. They were always five minutes early for the bus, because Allison couldn't afford for Marley to miss it.

If Marley didn't make it to the bus that meant Allison had to either drive Marley to school herself or they would both stay home for the day. Getting in the car and driving to school would be a shock to Marley, even if a small one. Shocks weren't good. Allison knew because she tried to drive Marley once, before this routine was carved in stone by lightning bolts sent from God himself. They had been running late; Allison watched as the bus sped down the road, not slowing and definitely not turning around.

Fine, she thought, and began walking Marley to the car.

The twelve year old girl was okay up until the moment that the car door opened, then both hands turned into fists and started whacking at the sides of her head. One at a time. Hard.

Left.

Right.

Left.

Right.

A doctor ended up having to leave the school to come sedate Marley. The girl never said a word, just attempted to beat the brains out of her head. Thus, if Marley missed the bus, Allison was staying home without even attempting to drive her daughter to school, and that meant Allison had to skip work, which was something they couldn't afford. Things were expensive, much more so now than when Jerry was alive and they possessed two incomes to float the bills. For one, the therapy Marley needed wasn't cheap, and two, the meds weren't either. Allison wasn't working for the FBI anymore, hadn't been since she found Marley in that gruesome warehouse. She now worked as a manager for an insurance company on the claims side. The work wasn't rewarding, but it had medical benefits and a 401k and paid better than nearly anything but banking. Allison had spent her previous life—her life with her husband and daughter—working on climbing a conceptual career ladder. Now, there was no ladder. She had her job, and she would never move up, or at least not substantially, because she wasn't willing to dedicate anything over forty hours a week to it. During those forty hours, she gave everything she had, but when those were up—everyone at her job knew not to call.

She could miss work, could take days off if she needed, but if she didn't *need* the day then she didn't want to take it. Because when she actually *needed* a day off, then by God, it better be there.

Marley was the one that actually *needed* the days, so Allison was forced to oblige. Watching her father die left scars on Marley that doctors couldn't see, let alone understand. Her mind was a place of silence now, that's what the doctors told Allison. A place where nothing went through it and nothing came out of it. Allison wasn't sure she believed that fully, and maybe that was just mother's love talking and maybe not. She thought Marley took in more than she let anyone know. So when Marley reacted to dressing before breakfast, Allison would have done a handstand had she been able.

Still, for the most part, Marley's mind *was* quiet and the reason stood out starkly: her mind wasn't able to handle the world Matthew Brand showed her, so it had shut down. Maybe it would come back one day. Maybe it would slowly open itself up to the possibility that all the death it witnessed before no longer existed.

Allison tried not to consider that part, the Matthew Brand part.

She considered Jerry all the time. He constantly filtered through her thoughts, both in waves of depression and in appreciation for everything that he gave her while alive.

Marley never left Allison's thoughts.

Matthew Brand, though, that was someone she didn't allow herself to think about. She received the call from the scientist four years ago; she knew Jeffrey Dillan and the woman he lived with were missing, presumed dead. Allison had allowed that knowledge to fill her with terror for a long time, terror that the escaped man had taken Dillan. That the escaped man, a black man who had raped numerous women before being caught, was actually filled with Brand's intellect, his personality. She lived in terror that eventually this black man with Brand's mind would come for her, would come for Marley, would come finish what he started with Jerry.

Nothing happened though. No one else turned up missing.

4

No cops died and Matthew Brand didn't resurface. There was a brief hunt after the scientist gave his proclamation, but it filtered down from the FBI that Brand was dead, that no one could have survived what the doctor claimed had happened. No one need worry about Matthew Brand because he was gone, finally. Allison believed that, but only because she didn't have a choice.

The alternative left her believing Brand was alive, and that wasn't something Allison could entertain. Not as a single mother raising a daughter whose mind was scarred by the lunatic. She couldn't add that onto her shoulders, not if she wanted to keep her collarbone from cracking. If Brand was alive after all these years, had he given up? Had he moved onto something else? Or was he biding time?

Those thoughts could take over her mind if Allison let them, so she didn't.

Marley finished her bowl of cereal and placed her spoon loudly onto the table. That was her way of saying she was finished, as well as Allison's way of knowing that her daughter wasn't as gone as the doctors claimed. Allison clicked the television off and stood up from the loveseat.

The man looked at her through the television's reflection. He was tall, over six-feet, and his body solid. Her breath caught in her lungs, her mouth hanging slightly open.

Allison Moore turned around and looked at a black man named Arthur Morgant, a rapist who had been sentenced to a frozen life twenty five years ago. His face was tilted down slightly, his eyes still looking at her. His skin was the deep brown of mahogany, but his eyes were the color of beautiful, deep blue.

"Hi, Agent Moore," Matthew Brand said.

For the first time in four years, Allison didn't think about her daughter, but ran instead—heading to her bedroom in hopes of making it there before he could.

* * *

Matthew watched Allison Moore take off to her right. She dashed for the hallway behind both of them, probably for a gun she kept somewhere back there. Matthew allowed himself a second to watch her go, a second to see her for the first time in years, but knew the time to watch was brief. If he slipped here, nothing else could possibly work. He allowed himself that moment of indulgence, but no more or everything to come might be ruined.

He raced after her, this body so different than the last one he owned. It contained a power that his frail frame hadn't approached before. His physical feats had only been completed by shock and audacity, but here, with these muscles covered in dark skin, he moved with an ease he hadn't known possible. His legs propelled him down the hallway, his strides catching up with Moore's quickly. He watched as she rounded a doorway, knowing she was approaching whatever she hunted. If she shot him, managed to call the police, if anything happened here besides him capturing her silently—plans would change drastically.

He turned the bedroom corner, and thank God and all His Host of Angels, she was reaching up to the top of her walk-in closet. She had locked her gun away and it couldn't help her now.

Matthew bombarded the closet, grabbing Allison's hair with his massive hand and then slamming her head into the corner of the door frame. She struggled, trying to fight her way back to the gun, trying somehow to overtake this hulk throwing her around.

Matthew slammed her head a second time.

And a third.

And, finally, Allison's body went slack.

Matthew dragged her by her hair, tossing her onto the floor in front of the bed. Her eye was already swelling; a gash on her forehead dripped blood across her face, combining with the blood running from her nose.

Matthew felt Morgant rising, felt the original owner of the body stretching forth with a fury Matthew hadn't known.

Take her. Take her. TakehertakeherTAKEHERTAKEHERTAKEHER.

"SHUT UP!" Matthew screamed into the empty room, his voice growling like bass from a sub-woofer.

The urge to penetrate, Morgant's voice, all of it welled inside Matthew, and though his pronouncement quieted it some, he could still feel Morgant desperately wanting to get back to the surface. Desperately wanting him to rip Moore's clothes off, then his own, and lay on top of her naked body, pumping up and down until he sprayed his seed everywhere. Matthew decided two years ago what his plans were, and now, somehow, Arthur Morgant was deciding he wanted a say in things. Not a say perhaps, but just a piece. His cut. His rapes.

Matthew looked down at the woman before him and couldn't state he didn't want to. Or that a part of him didn't want to. He wanted to dive down on top of her and take her, take her the way the memories in Morgant's head told him it could be. Part of him wanted that while the rest felt nothing but revulsion, a deep sickness that made him want to vomit.

Rape.

All of Matthew's murders came with a reason behind them. Even what would happen next for Moore and her daughter served a purpose. *These* thoughts had no purpose besides some primal desire Matthew had never known before—a desire stemming from Morgant's unconscious, still inside this body, if pushed way down. A purpose to please that desire, to satisfy it, which was no purpose at all.

*Takehertakeher,*the words whispered again to him.

No. He wouldn't. He didn't have time to think about this, to try and understand why it was happening. Matthew had felt these urges before, but they had been nothing, something he dismissed as a leftover ghost from the body he now owned. Something was happening inside him, something was changing, and he needed to figure out what, and if it could be stopped.

Not right now, though. Now he had to move Moore and her daughter.

* * *

Matthew walked back into the hallway.

Marley stood in it, her long hair hanging next to her face. Her body showed no signs of fear, no signs of any emotion at all.

The two of them stared at each other for a moment, Matthew wondering if she would wake up and realize who stood in front of her, or if she was too far gone for that. It didn't really matter, though; she would serve her purpose without ever having to think another thought.

"Hi, Marley. Glad to see you," Matthew said, and walked down the hall to collect the girl.

8

2

Two

Jake Deschaine looked at the phone he had just hung up. He knew there were things he needed to do, things that he should already be doing right now, even though the call only ended moments before. He needed to make sure he had the correct address. He needed to call a few sergeants, make sure they had their people heading out there. He needed to get in his own car, head to the scene, and probably call forensics on his way. There were things to do, and speed—as always—mattered.

Jake didn't move though. He just stared at the phone, listening to the words echo inside his head.

"The missing persons names are Allison and Marley Moore. Their house is at Fifty-Six Cherry Way. Beat cop went by because Moore's work said she had no-showed which was out of character. Should have uniforms getting there within the hour."

"The names again?"

"Allison Moore, and her daughter, Marley Moore."

"Them? Like, not people with similar names, but them?"

"As far as I know, yes."

Jake didn't know Allison Moore. Had never met the woman

and never seen her daughter. The name, though, was as common to Jake as Stephen King's would be to a fan of horror fiction. Four years ago the woman had been the most important law enforcement officer in the entire country. Jake had just started patrolling Katy, Texas back then, but he watched her press conferences and read every piece of news that he ran across. She practically disappeared as soon as the case ended, and the country knew why, because that killer, Matthew Brand, took everything from her. Jake heard she ended up moving to Katy, which made sense because of the children's clinic that the entire city touted as *the* best in the nation.

And now, Jake was what? Investigating her disappearance?

That's exactly what he was doing.

He didn't know the woman, had only seen her on television and online, and not even that in four years—but he still felt a loss. What had Allison Moore been to him? An idol? A goal? He hadn't been some impressionable sixteen year old when she began her search; he was twenty-four, yet still, she had left her mark. He watched her travel the country, watched her trying things that no one else would have even thought of. Then he watched her lose everything while still stopping that psychotic.

Except now, Jake was about to drive a car to her house and look into a missing persons report.

He stood up from his desk, grabbing his cell phone and placing it in his pocket. He'd give his dad a call on the way, if he had time. Jake felt like he'd woken up in some different dimension: a world that he didn't know and might not care to know. He wasn't supposed to be the one doing this, looking into the disappearance of someone who should be considered a national hero.

3

Three

If someone had asked Art Brayden what was wrong, he would have told them, "I'm fucking pissed."

No one asked though because no one here in Texas knew who he was or why he was here. He had shown up, more or less, on his own volition without giving warning to anyone. His boss knew—vaguely—and by vaguely it meant his boss thought Art was taking a few vacation days.

Art hadn't spoken with Allison Moore in years. If he thought hard about it, perhaps they last spoke six months after the whole shootout (which received just about as much media coverage as anything Art had ever seen). He asked her how Marley was doing, received some honest answers, and that had been it. Allison left the bureau and Art didn't, but he wasn't really expecting her to stay around anyway. Her husband was dead and her daughter nearly the same, a body without a mind wasn't much of a life, so it was clear to everyone that Allison had more pressing things to deal with than catching criminals. So. Three and a half years since he spoke to her? Four years since he'd seen her?

Last night he got the call that she was missing. It wasn't

anything huge, not anything the news would pick up if law enforcement had any luck. The call came to him because he had been her last boss at the bureau. It came to him because he'd been there with her when they shot holes through a metal warehouse and killed a monster. The FBI kept an eye on her, so when her job reported her missing and the cops showed up to an empty house, the FBI was made aware (even if most people involved didn't care too much) which filtered its way to Art Brayden.

Art cared, so when he heard, he took two days off and flew from Washington D.C. to Texas. He wasn't dropping anything off at a hotel room; he waited for a taxi at the airport, loaded his bag in the trunk, and told the driver Allison's address.

There wasn't any reason for Allison Moore to be missing. Her daughter either. They should be at work and school, but they weren't. No one knew where they were, and from what the call said last night, a splattering of Allison's blood was in the house.

It could be a copycat.

That's what Art kept saying to himself. Allison was missing but that didn't mean *he* was back.

This isn't some Harry Potter novel. You can say his name.

Art didn't want to though. He never wanted to say that name again, never wanted to even think it. Not out of fear, but out of the headaches that came with it. The man that shouldn't be alive, that *wasn't* alive—Art never wanted to chase him again. Chasing that man was like chasing a ghost, something that didn't exist except in your imagination. He didn't want to chase a ghost. He didn't want to go through it again. Art didn't fear him because Art only feared his creator, the Almighty God, and knew that one day God would lay this man as low as possible. God would take care of him in His own time and all the fear and hate that Brand had caused in the world would be put back on him. He knew that in the end everything would be taken care of without Art's help, but Art *still* didn't want to deal with the part that might need his help. The part of capturing the man.

Just say it.

Of capturing Matthew Brand.

It didn't matter, he wasn't alive. Dillan was dead, or at least gone, but that didn't mean Brand took him. It didn't mean that some superhuman, science-fiction creation had gobbled him up. It meant that the guy had done a lot of dirty deeds and someone finally offed him. Maybe they kidnapped him and took his money. Maybe Dillan fled on his own. None of it meant that Brand showed up and killed him; none of it meant he had done the same with Allison.

It could be a copycat.

Jesus, for fuck's sake, let it be a copycat.

There wasn't any other reason for Moore to be missing; Art kept finding himself at that inescapable truth. His mind traveled over and over the possible paths, and in the end, he came to that single answer. No one hated Allison Moore. No one really even knew she existed any longer. She had disappeared from the public eye quickly and was forgotten, which was what she wanted—a life of trying to fix her daughter. Except now she wasn't here anymore nor the daughter she dedicated herself to, and why? Brand, or a copycat, took her. No one else is stealing a woman with a handicapped child.

Art boarded a plane heading to Texas at five in the morning for two reasons. He felt somewhat responsible for this. Not completely; he wouldn't put that on himself, just as he hadn't put the responsibility for the last Brand disaster completely on Allison. The Lord said each man would account for his own sins, and so if Brand had shown up in Texas and taken away this woman, then Brand would pay for that one day. Art's responsibility lay with his forceful denial of Brand being alive. Three years ago, when that damned scientist started calling everyone he could about The Wall, saying Brand had escaped through someone else, Art called it preposterous. Ridiculous. Laughable. When Dillan turned up missing, Art discarded it as a coincidence at best and a publicity stunt by the writer at worst. Art had used a lot of clout to keep the bureau from looking. Allison told him once that he should do that anyway, that he should let Brand do as he pleased, get his son back, and then disappear from the world. Art didn't do it, obviously, because he followed the goddamn bastard to Florida and got a whole bunch of people killed in the process. So maybe that was part of the reason he pushed against anyone believing Brand still existed. The other part, though, was that Art didn't believe it. He understood that Brand had escaped from The Wall himself, that was *possible*, but that Brand had hidden himself inside the machine? Had then somehow implanted himself into one of the other criminals and *broke out again*? Insanity like that didn't exist. The other prisoner escaped the same way Brand had, because the whole idea of The Wall was idiotic and didn't possess the necessary technology to hold its prisoners in.

That's what he preached and that's what the world came to believe, at least the part of the world Art concerned himself with.

Allison was missing though, four years later, and no one had been watching out for her. The FBI only heard about it because her name tripped off alarms in their system. No cops sat outside her house. No one checked in periodically. Why would they? Brand was dead and no one besides him would hate this woman.

Only, Allison was missing.

It's a copycat. It's someone that wants to start scaring the entire country again, and the best way to do it was to grab her.

Art told himself that for the entire hour ride from the airport to Allison Moore's house.

* * *

Eighteen hours after the first cop showed up, the premises were still abuzz. Twenty police officers moved around the house, a few stood out on the driveway talking, and yellow police tape was strung up around the yard and driveway entrance. Art had a general idea of what all these people were doing, but it had been decades since he had to do any of it himself. He knew they were trying to figure out what happened, but didn't really understand the 'hows' behind it. He didn't need to anymore.

He got out of the taxi then draped his FBI ID around his neck. He rarely wore the necklace ID, but he simply didn't want to have to explain himself to everyone that asked. They might instead ask what the FBI cared about this, but maybe not. Either way, the FBI didn't care, not yet, and so he wasn't going to do much answering.

"Keep the meter running. I'm going to want to leave here in a bit, okay?"

The cab driver nodded, not saying anything, but gazed lazily out at the crime scene in front of him.

Art stepped over the tape and walked up the driveway. Local cops looked but didn't say anything. Art wasn't carrying a notepad, a gun, nothing. He was here to view the scene and hopefully leave with at least a semblance of surety that this had nothing to do with Brand.

He walked through the front door and stood in the foyer. The living room was to his right, the kitchen straight ahead, and a hallway towards his left.

"How did the intruder get in?" Art asked two cops standing in the living room.

They turned to him. "Excuse me?" One said.

Art lifted up his necklace, dangling it from a finger. "How did the intruder get in?"

The cop who had spoken nodded. "No signs of forced entry. No broken windows or door frames. The only damage to the house happened in the bedroom, where it looks like the perp bashed the victim's head against the closet door frame. We're really not sure how the perp gained entry yet, unless the victim let him or her in."

Art let his eyes drop to the living room floor. "Was she in here when things started?"

"We think so. Some of the furniture has been slightly moved which probably happened when she started running to get to the gun in the bedroom. She kept it locked in a box at the back of her closet."

A former FBI agent who kept her gun locked up and hidden in a closet. A former FBI agent who had once been hunted by the goddamn devil deciding she no longer needed a weapon around her and her daughter. So stupid. Art wanted to shake her right now, just grab her by her shoulders and shake her until her teeth clapped against each other inside her head. Had she kept the gun within eyesight, she probably would still be here. She and her daughter.

"Thanks," Art said and walked into the kitchen. He looked at the small table with two chairs underneath it. A box of cereal stood next to a bowl. Art walked over and looked inside; it was mostly empty besides a thin layer of colored milk at the bottom. The food-dye from the cereal had leaked into the milk, giving it a slightly green color. Nothing had been touched in the house yet. Soon Allison's family would begin arriving and they would take things out and the box of half-full cereal would find itself thrown into a garbage can. For now, nothing was disturbed because the police had no bodies, no perpetrators, no breaking and entering. They had a missing person and were hoping something in this house would give them a clue as to what happened yesterday morning.

Art turned from the kitchen and started walking down the hallway. Someone passed on his left but didn't look at him or give any salutation. Art had been told what was in the bedroom, but he wanted to see it for himself. Just because there was a message didn't mean it was Brand. It didn't mean anything besides someone had written something. Grandiose actions were copycat killer trademarks

They're also Brand's trademarks.

He walked into the bedroom and his eyes were drawn to a detective squatting down over a bloodstain. Art moved over to it, standing a few feet back from the cop, but still able to see the scarlet red on the white carpet. Not a lot of blood, just enough to be noticeable.

The detective looked up. "Heard you might be stopping by. My name is Jake Deschaine." The man extended his hand and Art left it there for a second.

"Heard I'd be stopping by?"

"Yes, sir. Kind of a rumor that's been going around, saying someone from the FBI might take an interest and you were the most likely candidate." Jake's hand still hung in the air.

Art shook it, then looked back down at the stain on the carpet, saying nothing else.

"There's blood here and then you'll find some in the closet

17

smeared on the inside of the frame. She was trying to grab the gun from up above, but it's lying on the floor now, in its case, unopened. She got pretty close to it, apparently."

"Someone up front said you don't know how the perp got in?" Art asked as he walked to the closet.

"Nothing official, but I'm pretty sure he came through a window in here." Jake pointed next to the bed. "The left window isn't locked but the right one is, which doesn't make a lot of sense. Of course, the victim could have slept on one side or the other and opened one window or the other, but why she would do that during a Texas summer is beyond me. The rest of the windows in the house are locked too."

Art found the window and looked at the latch. "So, then, how did this one become unlocked?"

"At some point, the perp had to have access to the house. That's the only thing that makes sense if the theory holds. He came in, unlocked the window, and left again."

"Why not just take her then or come in the same way the next time?"

"Because this window is facing the backyard would be my biggest guess. The front door was locked when we arrived, and the only other door to the house actually exits on the side that faces a neighbor, with a stone pathway that leads to the backyard. That door was locked, too. So it would be hard for the perp to come in the front door and drag people out that way. Someone would have seen. He arrived when no one was home, unlocked the window, and then left. He came back later, I don't know how much later, when people were home and came through the window, then took everyone out the window as well."

Art nodded. He wasn't sure if any of what the kid said was

true, but it made some logical sense. Art walked back to the closet, having gone to the window before getting a chance to look inside it.

"The blood is smeared in a consistent pattern with someone getting their head whacked on the wall a few times. You can see where the original blood splatter happened here, and then as the perp continued to hit her, how it smeared as her face continually touched the wood."

Art looked over to the gun case on the floor. Two feet and a combination password away from safety. That's how close Allison had been to staying alive. Or maybe she was still alive, just in serious pain. That was Brand's modus operandi, wasn't it? He hadn't been able to kill any of the people previously because he needed them alive to create his ghastly experiments. *Except, in his mind, there weren't any experiments happening. To Brand, the theory was reality, all he had to do was walk through the steps.*

That would be the worst, if she was in some kind of suspended state, not dead, not alive, perhaps knowing the same fate awaited her daughter.

"And then on the wall above the bed..."

Art stopped listening to the detective. He hadn't wanted to look there yet. He had purposefully avoided looking above the headboard, because he didn't want to see the message. He didn't want to face the possible implications, and maybe he had tried to hide that from himself earlier, but he couldn't now. Art needed prayer and while he might hide things from himself, he couldn't hide anything from God.

Give me the strength, Father. God didn't always listen, especially to Art, and he understood that. Put simply, God had a lot to do, and worrying about Art—with his foul mouth and temper—well that couldn't always be at the top of His list. Maybe now though, this one time, God could alter His plans just a bit and listen. Because this shit might get difficult.

Art looked up at the bed and saw the maroon streaks which looked almost like a child's finger painting—besides the message.

The question read: *How about we stop with the nonsense and end all this?*

* * *

"There's nothing here. I mean nothing. This detective feels pretty sure whoever broke in came through the bedroom window, but other than that—nothing. No DNA. No forced entry. Just Moore's blood dabbled in a few places," Art said into his cellphone.

"And the scribbling on the wall?"

Art sighed. "Well, by nothing, I meant nothing besides that. That is, unfortunately, a pretty fucking big something. They managed to get some partial prints and it checks out as a ninety-eight percent match with Arthur Morgant."

"How do you feel about having the same name as someone who is going to be famous for horrible crimes?"

Art didn't smile. "Man. Fuck. What do we do?"

"Elegant as always, Art," Gyle James said. "How are the media stations down there playing it?"

"There've been a few stories, nothing major. They mainly just mention that Moore was involved in the Brand case a couple years back."

A few seconds of silence came over the phone before Gyle said, "Arthur Morgant, that's the escapee right? The one you told us couldn't possibly be Brand. That one we didn't need to worry about?"

"That would be him."

"Just as long as you know I went to bat for you back then. So don't say anything stupid this time because I can't go to bat twice in this game."

"I know," Art said.

"There's nothing else down there? No other signs of what might have happened? Why she was taken? What the message means? Where Morgant is? Nothing?"

"No. She's gone. Her daughter's gone. The house is empty and no one is hanging out that shouldn't be. Family comes in tomorrow to begin gathering things. The police are questioning neighbors, but there isn't a lot to use right now."

"Who's in charge?"

"The detective I told you about. Jake something or other."

"Okay, stay with him for the next few days. I'm going to get some analysts on this and see what we can find out if we start looking cross country."

"Yes, sir," Art said.

"I'll give you a call tonight."

Art waited hours on the call before falling asleep, phone next to him and silent.

4

Four

The moonlight always fell down out here as if the heavens were trying to speak with Matthew. He had reveled in the beauty of science's creations, marveled at the genius of an electron collider or a telescope. But here, in this place, the moon struck him just as powerfully; he saw it as gorgeous. It turned everything into a black and white hue and cast shadows all the way from the smallest blade of grass to the lighthouse he had come to visit.

He could only visit at night, so he was never able to see the place during daylight, but it was still something to behold now, for sure.

Matthew walked from his van across the graveled driveway and to the bottom of the lighthouse. The structure stood so tall, and yet the door he entered through was barely big enough to allow him in. He found the key in his pocket and twisted open the lock. Stepping inside, he left the beauty of nature for the beauty of his mind.

He hit a light switch and the building illuminated, cascading upwards in a series of rings.

He had two new additions, but he wanted to get a look before he started working. That's what this came down to: work. What stood before him was work. What came next was work. His whole life, except for maybe the early years where he half listened to his professors and stayed inside his own head, had been work. There was a lot left to do, *a lot*, but soon all his work would end. He could finally rest and place down the yoke he had thrown on his shoulders all those years ago. He wanted a second just to admire this though, just a moment. It would grow much greater, without any doubt, but even now, he thought it rivaled everything produced by any other mind, ever. Isaac Newton, Albert Einstein, Leonardo Da Vinci—none of them could look on what stood before Matthew and say they could have done better.

It took Matthew two years to figure out that God had a sense of humor. Two years of struggling with the design, of not being able to create what his mind said was possible. Staring at a notepad, scribbling down formulas, sitting in a shitty Texas apartment with the heat having no end, he finally understood the reason he wasn't able to extract the power he wanted: he was positioning the bodies wrong. The feet needed to be placed over one another. The arms outstretched. The bodies needed to resemble a dying Christ. From that realization, the whole structure before him was born, and he began building.

He had removed the steps that once wound their way upward along the edge of the lighthouse's wall. Matthew hollowed out the building and then replaced it with his own ideas. A large pole stood implanted into the ground, shooting all the way to the top of the lighthouse, to where a light once burned for ships. Surrounding this pole, supported by beams sticking outward from it, were large, circular rings. The largest was at the bottom, and every ten feet, another (and smaller) ring was added. Until at the very top, the smallest ring had been placed, and Matthew thought he might be able to attach two people on it. If he was wrong though, and off one person, everything would still work. To be honest, his plans were a bit overkill. Better safe than sorry and all that, plus, Matthew was never short on dramatics.

Right now, he had two bodies attached to the rings and two more waiting in his car.

Jeffrey Dillan, and the woman who decided living with him would be a good idea, hung above Matthew. They had been hanging for the past two years, and looked nothing like the people he originally brought in here. Those people had been lean, fit, hair trimmed, alert. The people before him could barely be identified as human.

Their hair had passed far beyond their shoulders. Dillan's beard continued to grow, reaching his collarbone now. The once fit muscles were all flab, looking like they were melting from the bones. Their hands were splayed out to the side, their feet lay one over the other, mimicking Christ on the cross. Matthew had designed it that way on purpose. It lent itself for a nice bit of irony, he thought. Metal poles connecting back to the ring passed through each of their hands, another through their feet.

Matthew walked over to Jeffrey Dillan, suspended ten feet in the air, his body naked. Two wires sprang from the pupils of his eyes and into the bolts drilled through his hands. The same for his girlfriend that hung beside him. A large tube ran from each of their mouths, down the outside of their bodies and across the floor to a giant barrel. Liquid food was pumped from the barrel once a day, containing all the nutrients that these two—as well as the two in the car—would ever need. The food supply was self-generating, pretty much. Like a compost pile, but one for humans rather than plants.

24

Jeffrey was still alive, which Matthew enjoyed almost as much as anything else. Everyone that hung on these giant rings would be alive for as long as it took to fill this light-tower. Right now, Jeffrey felt the pain of wires feeding through his eyeballs and into the soft tissue of his brain beneath. When food came through the tubes, filling up his esophagus, and spilling over his mouth because he couldn't swallow fast enough, he knew it.

Jeffrey deserved it. Matthew had *heard* Hilman's voice. He had heard it for the briefest of seconds and then everything had been shattered. Everything he worked twenty years for, everything he had come so close to capturing, had been stolen from him. They destroyed his mind, and then his body. Dillan made that possible, because Dillan's lust for money allowed him to tail Matthew for months, allowed him to understand everything about the operation Matthew amassed.

At the end, though, Dillan lost his nerve and ratted.

Matthew heard Hilman's voice and then heard it no more. All because of the man hanging before him. So, yes, Dillan deserved it. He deserved to hang here until his skin rotted from his bones and only a skeleton remained. Unfortunately, Matthew wouldn't be able to give him what he deserved, because there wasn't enough time for that.

He had a lot of work to do tonight, hanging up the woman and child that were in the van outside wouldn't be easy. Tomorrow, he had his coming out party, as he thought of it. The time for thought was over, at least for tonight.

It was now time for action.

* * *

"I only spoke with Agent Moore once besides the brief words I said before taking her. Kind of a, 'hey, nice to see you thing'.

I thought that I might speak to you a bit more. We're going to be in this together, I think, but I'm not running away this time. I'm not searching for any of your law enforcement friends, so the chances of us ever actually meeting face to face is nil. And thus, I thought I'd give you a call. You can run the trace, but the analysts aren't going to track anything. Do the cops in Texas have that kind of sophistication anyway? I doubt it, but I'll wait if you need to plug your cellphone up to anything."

All Art said was hello, and he had been answered with an almost stream of conscious one-way conversation.

"Who is this?" He asked, his cellphone still against his ear.

"My body is Arthur Morgant's, the same one the cops you're with probably fingerprinted from Moore's house. My mind is who I've always been though, Matthew Brand."

Art tried to swallow although his mouth had suddenly filled with cotton balls.

"How did you get my number?" Art asked.

"I looked it up online. I've worked on projects a lot harder than the ability to look up strangers' phone numbers, Art."

Art stood up and rushed across the room to Jake's desk. He tapped the younger man on the shoulder and started pointing at his phone.

It's him, he mouthed.

"Art, take your time. I'm in no rush. Get your people involved; I'll be here."

Fuck it then, Art thought. "It's him. Brand, he's on my phone. Can you guys track this?"

Jake bolted up from his chair. "Umm...no, not under this short notice." He looked around for a second and then grabbed a notepad and pen. "Put it on speakerphone." He sat back down and started typing into his computer, hammering out words, suddenly blind to everything else around him. "I'm going to try to get someone in here to trace it, and I'm going to contact your cellphone provider. Who do you have?"

Art held the phone a few inches from his ear. "Verizon," he said, not understanding at all what the kid was doing.

"Hey, somebody get over here!" Jake shouted into the air, his fingers nearly breaking the sound barrier as he hammered on the keyboard. "You two," he said at the cops walking over. "Take down every bit of the conversation that is about to happen. Every bit. Pens and paper right there," he said, nodding to his desk.

"Sounds like everything is good on your end, Art. Ready to talk?"

Art looked around the police station. Twenty or thirty people in here and only three of them over at this desk ready to listen to what might be the most important professional conversation any of them ever heard. Or maybe it was bullshit. Just because someone said they were Matthew Brand didn't make it so. For Art, he wasn't comfortable with this. He wasn't a negotiator. He wasn't from Texas. He wasn't a field operator anymore. Hadn't been for fifteen years. He *managed* field operations. He developed strategy. He didn't talk to psychos on phones and try to decipher what they meant. And here was this twenty-something computer geek, apparently, taking charge as if he'd been waiting for the call. Jake still hadn't looked up from the screen as he frantically tried to get someone here who could install tracking software. The other two cops were looking at him now, waiting on him to do something, and he felt like he didn't exactly know what to do. Talk to this guy? Talk to the man with the deep voice who claimed to have the mental state of the smartest man to ever live?

27

"How do I know you are who you say you are?" Art asked. He turned the speaker on and laid his phone on the desk.

"Well. That's a good question. I guess I hadn't really figured you might think someone else took Moore, but it makes sense. Did you ever check out the crime scene notes or photos from Dillan's disappearance?"

Art had. He'd looked at them for hours, had considered even flying to California to look at the house himself. "Yeah," Art answered.

"His tongue was in the sink. The kitchen sink. No papers spoke about that. No Fox News' report mentioned it. I cut it out for obvious reasons."

Art remembered the piece of meat sitting on the white basin, surrounded by blood and looking like some kind of small, dead, sea animal. The cops managed to keep that piece of the whole crime quiet, but... "Something else. That wasn't the only thing not allowed out to the public."

"I can't tell if you really don't believe me or actually think you might be able to get a trace on my location if you keep me talking long enough. Either is fine. You got a piece of my shoe print in the house. It was from the woman's blood, when I dragged her in from the balcony where she had been tanning. Her nose was bleeding and I stepped in it, the right edge of my right foot. It wouldn't be enough to identify my size, but you could definitely see the tracks. I remember looking at it but decided against wiping anything down because I knew no one would be seeing me for a while."

Art saw the photo in his mind. They had tried to determine the type of shoe, but it was a dead end.

"At the very least, you have to know I'm the one that took Jeffrey Dillan. You can believe I'm Matthew Brand or someone else if you want, and you can question whether or not I took Moore, but you must believe that I took Dillan."

Art looked at the two men scribbling on their pads of paper. Neither of them looked up or took a second to pause. Jake was staring at the phone, listening. Art noticed other people had gathered around. Everyone in the room was slowly migrating over to watch Art Brayden talk with the supposed perpetrator, and Art had no clue what to say. No idea what this conversation was about. No idea what to do at all. A man with thirty years of law enforcement experience and somehow he lost it all in the five minutes he'd been on the phone.

"Where's Moore?" He asked.

"She's with me. Or, rather, I know where she is. You needn't worry about her. You won't be getting her back, and if you did, her days of taking care of her daughter, or her daughter needing to be taken care of for that matter, are over. She's in God's hands now. Do you believe in God, Art?"

"I was baptized Catholic."

"When was the last time you took communion?"

"At mass this past Sunday."

"A true believer then!" Matthew shouted. "I think God is going to sit this one out, though, Art. To stop me, it would take a real intervention, I can tell you that."

"Stop you from doing what?"

"You were there when I died, weren't you? You and Moore?"

"Yes."

"You heard my son speak then, didn't you? You heard him ask me what was going on?"

Art closed his eyes. He didn't like thinking about that part. They had saved a young girl and ended a madman's killing spree. And at the same time, they had killed what sounded like a young man, someone who had no idea where he was or what was going on. They had killed him by destroying the glass house he was born into.

"I heard him," Art said.

"I can't remember his voice, because that body and mind died. I had to read about it in Dillan's book, unfortunately. However, I'm glad you told the truth; I'd hate to hear a man of God lie. Art, I've given up my chase for Hilman. I've realized that no matter what I do, you, your world, won't let me have him back. You'll fight me at every turn. You've taken everything in this world I had. My career. My son. My wife. My own body. I lost that battle and it took me being reborn into this body to understand. I get it now and I'm at peace. I'm not here for my son any longer. I'm here for the world, Art. I'm here to end all of your lives as you so effectively ended mine."

Art paused and seconds passed. He found Jake's eyes, and the kid was squinting, not fully in the present, but somewhere inside his own head.

"You're going to kill everyone in the world. That's what you're saying?"

"Exactly. You. The cops next to you. The people farming rice patties in North Korea. They're all going to die over the next couple of months."

"You planning on purchasing a few nukes? Terrorists have been trying that for years; we have some pretty sophisticated ways of stopping them."

Matthew laughed. "Moore thought a lot differently than you, didn't she? I don't think you're dumb, per se, maybe just too old to be involved in this. I won't be using nukes, Art."

"Enough with the bullshit. What do you want?" Art asked, his temper finally igniting. The man on the other end of this phone—Morgant, Brand, or some other psycho—was fucking around. He was saying shit just to say it, and none of it led anywhere. The guy was getting off on this, and Art stood here with his hand on the man's dick, just jacking him off.

"I want you to tell the world what's coming. That's all. Will you do that for me?"

"And what is coming? Because all I can see is that I'm going to catch you if you are who you say you are."

Matthew chuckled. "Would I call you if I thought there was even the remotest chance of that? It doesn't matter. Hear me out, and when I'm done, I want you to tell the world what I've told you, okay? I imagine within three months, there won't be a single living thing on this planet. I may be overstating my case, because there might be some life in the bottom of the oceans or underneath the Earth's surface, but not much more than that. I'm going to kill the sun, Art. Do you know how much energy rests inside a human body? Seventy trillion suns' worth. All of it tied up inside our atoms, most of the time unable to be released. I'm going to release it though, Art, and not just the energy in one body, but the energy in fifty-five bodies. I'm going to fire all of that energy directly at the sun, and then, I'm going to watch as it explodes. It may burn us out in a sort of supernovae explosion, or it may simply die, leaving a black mass floating in space. I'm hoping it's the black mass route, and I think it will be. That way humanity sits here for a few weeks in complete darkness, before they rot away. If it's a supernovae type thing, that'll be fine too. Everyone will feel a good bit of pain before life ends here. Do you understand what I'm saying, what I want you to communicate? I'm going to end the sun and that's going to end life here on Earth. Can you get that to some news stations or maybe up on a website somewhere?"

31

Art stared at the phone lying on the desk. The two men with pens in their hands had stopped writing. Art didn't look up to see what Jake was doing.

He didn't believe any of it. Not just the destruction of the sun, but the fact that someone was sitting here telling him they could accomplish such a feat, and expecting him to go along.

Art laughed. He put his hands on the desk, leaned over the phone, closed his eyes, and just laughed.

"No, motherfucker. I'm not putting that up on any website. Not because I don't want to do your bidding, but because I'm not going to lose my job over some farce. You may have taken Moore, you may have taken Dillan, but that's all you can do, Brand. Hell, you may be able to bring your son back, and ya know what? It seems like you have the amount of people needed to do it if my math is right. So all the power to you there. But what you can't do is stop the sun from shining. So quit with the bullshit."

Art listened as a sigh came through the phone. "How many times do I have to show you people? Why make this so hard?" He paused and no one on Art's side said anything. "Fine. Since you're a believer in The Christ, I'm going to do something for you until you do what I'm asking—I'm going to crucify someone publicly every day until my story is run nationally, that I'm going to end the world. You there, Art? I want to make sure you hear this. A crucifixion a day until you wise up. Talk soon."

The phone went dead.

5

Five

A crucifix was harder to make than Matthew originally thought. He had been able to build a machine which basically crushed human atoms and then directed them as a weapon into space, but here he was, trying to keep these two boards from swiveling around on one another. He finally put four more nails through the top board and that kept it from moving. Even so, he wished he had promised to do something else.

The woman lay across the board now, dead. He'd taken a simple drill bit and went through her skull into her brain. The pain was pretty excruciating for her at first, but ended quickly. He couldn't use a gun, because she needed to look as whole as possible for the greatest effect. So he used the drill, placing the woman's head in a vice and simply bearing down until the swirling piece of metal sank into her brain.

Matthew grabbed a nail, or rather, Matthew's relatively new, strong, black hands grabbed a nail. He placed it in the center of her hand and gently began sinking it into her flesh with tiny swings of his hammer.

Without a doubt, this was a waste of time. He needed to be hanging bodies inside the lighthouse, not hanging them on crosses so he could decorate the city.

His plan involved murder, involved inflicting his own pain back on the world. That was only part of it though, because he wanted the people of Earth to understand a few other things. The first was fear. He wanted the entire world to wait, knowing they could do nothing, hoping that if they hugged their loved ones they could stop it, thinking about their entire species' impending doom. He also wanted the world to know that *he* was doing it. When the sun stopped burning and darkness descended across the entire world, he didn't want a single person on this rock to wonder why. They needed to understand that he had done it, and the reason he had done it was because they took everything else from him. They gave him nothing, had effectively banded together as one society to say that Matthew Brand and everything he wanted did not matter. Hell, they even put him in a freezer for ten years just in case they needed his brain. They had no need for Matthew the person, though. That was clear. So they denied him his son and took his wife as well, and now they would know what came from that. He would take all of their wives and sons. He would take their grandkids and everyone they held dear. Their pets. Their walks in the park. He was going to steal all of their lives and all of the lives of the unborn.

For them to know that this was *his* plan—that when the sun stopped shining, *he* had done it—he needed officials to make an announcement. Matthew knew that part would be hard; no one simply gave terrorists what they wanted. So, he needed to show them that if they didn't do what he said, there would be a different kind of terror on their hands. He was only taking women, and they would hang from wooden boards all around the city until Art Brayden and his boss decided to listen. Matthew

34

would do it once a day for the next two weeks, and if they hadn't done their part by then, he would receive his first shipment of people to hang up in his lighthouse, and then he would start back with the crucifixes.

There were two rules to this game: the world would end, and the world would know he ended it.

Matthew was a simple man.

* * *

The sun rose over the buildings in downtown Boston as it had every morning for the past two hundred years. It rose, chasing away the darkness and trying its best to chase away some of the cold.

The priest always opened the doors to the church at the same time. Monday through Sunday, he made sure the doors were open to the public just as the sun peeked its head over the building across the street from the cathedral. He had done it for the past ten years and he had no plans to quit. He enjoyed opening the doors because it gave him solitude with the image of Christ for a few moments before others began their daily pilgrimage to give thanks and ask forgiveness.

The priest stepped from his car, which he parallel parked every day, unless someone stole his spot—which happened more than he would prefer. He looked down at his shoes, hoping he hadn't scuffed them on his drive in. It wasn't so much vanity, but that he didn't want to bring anything but his best before the Lord each day he served. They looked good, though, so he reached back into the car and grabbed his messenger bag.

He closed the door and walked ten feet before stopping.

It was the first time in ten years he had ever stopped on his way to opening the doors.

"Oh, dear God," he whispered.

A naked woman was plastered on the doors before him. She hung—literally hung as her body sagged down and her arms stretched upwards—on two pieces of wood. A cross, which leaned up against the doors the priest had arrived to unlock. Nails or something like them were shoved through both of her hands; her feet were crossed and a large stake had been driven through them. Blood pooled beneath her body, drying slowly. The blood appeared to have stopped dripping, although her hands and feet were smeared with it. Her head hung limply on her chest, her breasts lying lifelessly without any outward movement of breath from her lungs.

The priest crossed himself.

Then he collapsed and vomited on the sidewalk. It took another thirty minutes before someone walked by and saw both bodies.

The cops were finally called.

* * *

Art stared over his desk at Jake.

The kid was typing away at the computer; his fingers moving like the keys were merely an extension of his body rather than separate entities.

It was time to go home, or rather, to Art's office. Home was a long way off, probably. A lot more nights were going to be spent away from home over the next few months.

Brand. Art now thought the man who had called him could only be Matthew Brand. He wasn't thinking about him as a copycat. He wasn't thinking about him as Arthur Morgant, the rapist. Art finally believed that the man on the other side of the phone yesterday had been Matthew Brand. The street camera which recorded the drop off of the crucifix at the Catholic church (*and what a nice choice of venue, Matthew*) showed a black man, tall

36

and strong, pulling the cross (with the woman already attached) out of the van and then dragging it to the building. The guys in DC examined the video every which way, and they were ninety percent positive Arthur Morgant was the person in the video. And that meant, according to that scientist all those years ago, Brand was controlling Morgant's body.

And here was this kid, Jake—he knew that Brand put the body at that Catholic church in Boston, knew that the FBI was already moving in on his turf quite quickly, and yet here he was at the office, looking at photos and calling neighbors. Here he was, still working. Art had watched him over the past few days with a curiosity he didn't normally have for people. The kid was smart, flat out. The way he handled the call yesterday, when Art was almost shitting his pants, showed he had some leadership capabilities too. He seemed to understand the case as well, although Art hadn't asked him how. He could have read the books, but it was more than that. The books centered on Brand, and this kid knew about Allison. He knew about Allison's husband.

He even knew a relatively good bit about the science that allowed Brand to force himself into Morgant. Relatively being compared with Art's complete lack of knowledge.

"How do you know all that shit?" Art had asked.

"They wrote tons of articles about it when it first happened, even in Popular Science."

"Say it again, and dumb it down some."

Jake had smiled, making him look even younger than twenty-eight. "The Wall, it was like, the smartest computer ever built. You remember that computer which beat all the world championship chess players? Think like that, but on steroids. You can program a computer with almost anything you want.

Brand was in there so long, he simply programmed a piece of The Wall to be as near a replica of himself as he could create. It's not Brand in the sense that Brand was alive in there, it's Brand in that all his knowledge, his preferences, his history was uploaded into a single file. They have a few theories of how he got out of there, but the most likely thing is, he gave it a timed activation. It didn't matter if you guys killed him or not, Morgant was going to be filled with that file sooner or later, and Brand did that as a fail-safe, I imagine. If you guys killed him, which was a good possibility, he wouldn't be gone. If you didn't kill him, well, he could deal with Morgant when that time came."

"But how did he just take over Morgant?"

Jake nodded, looking away, gathering his thoughts. "The brain is nothing like a computer, so no one is really sure exactly how he made it happen. He might not even have known if it would work, might have only suspected or did it out of some kind of desperation. They think though, the brain took to it like it does with any new information it's fed—it tried to absorb it, and at some point, the data that made up Brand took over."

Art still didn't really understand it, but the kid did.

What are you trying to get at here? Art asked himself.

He wanted to know whether he was going back to DC alone, or whether Jake Deschaine should come with him. The detective was smart, capable, knowledgeable about the case, and the motherfucker worked. What did Art have now? Directives from his boss, and that was about it, so bringing in someone wouldn't hurt. They would need anyone that could contribute, and this guy could.

"Why not?" Art asked himself. "If he says no, so what."

Art stood from his desk and walked to Jake's cubicle.

38

"What's up?" Jake said, a phone in between his ear and his shoulder.

"You got a second?" Art asked.

Jake frowned a bit, but nodded, hanging up the phone. "What can I help you with?"

"Heard back from my boss today. We talked about Boston. I imagine you've figured it out, but you're done here. This whole office is off the case and you guys are going to go back to whatever the most pressing thing is for Katy, Texas police officers and detectives. I don't say that to be insulting, I just want you to know what your boss is going to be telling you in the next hour."

Jake nodded. "Yeah, most likely."

"So, I'm heading back to D.C. in a few hours. I'm about to go to my hotel, put my shit in my bag, and get to the airport. Do you want to come with me?"

Jake leaned back in his chair. "With you? To DC?"

"Yeah. To DC. The President is meeting with all the directors of every law enforcement agency in the country today. He's called scientists too. They're trying to see if what Brand told us yesterday is even remotely possible. If it isn't, then we're going to deal with this the same way we would any other crime. If it is, then we're going to have to figure out another plan. I'd like you on my team either way. You think you'd want to go?"

Jake leaned back in his chair and said, "Yeah, man. I'll go. What time is the flight?"

* * *

Jake folded a shirt and tossed it into the open suitcase sitting on his bed. He was almost packed and the cab would be here in thirty minutes to take him to the airport—and then what? Then he would get on a plane with the Director of Operations for the FBI and...become an FBI agent? Stay a detective for Katy, Texas? He didn't know but you didn't ask questions like that when the Director of Operations said he wanted you to come along. When that happened, one simply went along.

How long had he been complaining about his current boss to his father? A year? His newest promotion had put him under the prick—Bradley Vestor, and while he wouldn't have turned down the promotion if he knew what it meant, he still didn't like the person he worked under. In fact, he might venture far enough to say that he hated the man, Vestor. *Brad.* Even now, packing to head to Washington D.C. with Art Brayden, Jake couldn't stop thinking about how bad he wanted to get away from the Vestor. So whether or not he knew exactly what his position was going to be when he got to DC, at least he wouldn't be listening to the incompetence of Vestor on a weekly basis. Even this case, up until the call from Brand, Vestor said that it wasn't him. That it couldn't be him. That it was a copycat, and the leads Jake followed were dead-ends and he should stop them immediately. Jake didn't listen because Vestor was a coward more than anything. He'd bitch and complain, but he wouldn't do anything to stop Jake from following the case as he saw fit. The truth was, Vestor didn't *want* it to be Brand. He didn't even want to consider the possibility that such a responsibility might be thrown on him. Vestor coasted and that was something else Jake hated. Jake hadn't coasted to this high of a position in six years on the police force, he'd busted ass, but now he was under a man who thought the road to heaven was probably still being paved because working slow was almost akin to righteousness.

So there was that; he'd be able to call and tell his father that he wasn't working for Vestor anymore. He thought Brayden was sharp too; he'd watched him over the past few days, watched

how he worked, what he did, what he said. He saw the man slip
briefly when Brand first called, but would Jake have behaved any
differently? Would anyone, if someone claiming to be Matthew
Brand called their phone without any notice? He didn't think so,
and even if Brayden slipped there for a second, the man hadn't
slipped anywhere else. So yeah, Jake didn't know exactly what
was going to happen when he got out to DC, but it had to be
better than sitting here under Vestor and working on the next
7-11 robbery. Which was coming. You could bet on that in Katy.

Jake tossed a pair of khakis into the suitcase and walked to
his closet to grab his suits. Did they wear suits in the FBI? He
had to imagine they weren't walking around in khaki pants all
day. Either way, it didn't matter—they had a Brooks Brothers
in DC if his suits weren't up to snuff.

Matthew Brand. That's who they were going after. That's
who *he* was going after. What had his plans been before this?
To continue working his way up and maybe, if he had a lot of
luck, reach Chief one day? Maybe to apply for the FBI down
the road and see where that took him? In a single week he'd
been recruited by a man who was two steps away from the
President though. What had Moore thought when she got the
first call about Brand? When she was told to suit up because
she was about to chase the smartest man in the world? Jake
was sitting here happy, mainly to be getting away from Vestor,
but there were some nerves coming into play too. He wasn't
being recruited because he had a great jawline; they wanted
him to produce. Maybe not to the level Moore had been at, but
still, Brayden must have thought Jake would be able to bring
something that others couldn't. So that's what he needed to
do, to produce value. He'd done it before, not on this scale
obviously, but he had put sixteen cases in the black over the

past three years and that wasn't anything to shy away from. Sixteen cases in three years tied for the county's best, and he did it at twenty-eight years old. The other detective was forty-five.

"Produce, produce, produce," Jake said absently, picking up his shoes.

This was, without a doubt, a great opportunity.

6

Six

"That's all you saw, Father?"

"Son, I've told the police everything. I do not understand why you feel the need to question me again. Let the police do their job and you and I will do ours."

Joe looked at the old Mexican and said nothing for a few seconds. He knew he was lucky the priest hadn't asked him to leave as soon as he started asking questions; he also knew that the priest could just as easily let the cops know a civilian was snooping around. Wondering things he had no business wondering

"Do you know who I am, Father?"

"No."

"My name is Joseph Welch. Have you ever heard of me?"

The priest looked down at his lap. Both men sat next to each other on benches in front of the stone engraved sculpture of Jesus hanging from the cross. Joe kept his eyes on the priest, not caring about any of the surroundings, not caring about the fact that he was in God's house. He had come here because the priest had seen the crucifix. He would next go to the person who actually called and reported it to the police. Joe knew everything

The Boston Herald had said about the dead woman, and now he wanted to know if the priest knew anything the paper didn't.

"I remember your name. I prayed for you years ago when you were in the newspaper. I prayed that you might find peace. Have you found it?"

"No. There's no peace left for me here."

"Have you searched for it?" The priest asked.

"What do you think I'm doing now, Father?"

"Whatever you're doing, there is no peace at the end of it." The priest looked back to his lap. "I saw nothing else but what the paper told you. I saw the woman hanging in mockery of our Lord, and then I collapsed. There was nothing else to see. There was nothing else I wanted to see."

Joe stood from the pew. "Thank you."

He left the priest sitting by himself as he walked from the cathedral.

* * *

Joe had known it would start again. He knew it the moment the world said Brand escaped a second time. He knew it when Dillan disappeared and he knew it these past two years when no one else even thought about Matthew Brand. Joe knew Brand wasn't done. Knew that he couldn't be done and that he would return bringing all his havoc and hellfire with him. Joe kept tabs on everyone. Art Brayden. Allison Moore. The judge from Brand's trial. He kept up to date with anyone that might be a target, because when Matthew Brand decided to come back, Joe Welch was determined to be ready.

Matthew Brand had finally returned, although only a few people knew it. When Allison Moore disappeared a few days ago, an alert came through on Joe's email because a few local news stories were printed in a small Texas town. Joe left his house that morning, caught a flight with only one bag packed, and went to Texas. He didn't need to be there long. He used a rental car to drive by Moore's house, or former house, and when he saw Art Brayden standing out on the driveway, Joe knew all he needed. Art Brayden wasn't showing up to any missing person's house unless something big was happening. That something had to be Matthew Brand. There wasn't anyone else that would take Moore and her daughter.

Joe would still be in Texas but for the crucifix in Boston.

No one in media made the connection, but Joe didn't need them to. Moore missing in Texas and two days later a dead woman nailed to a cross shows up in Boston. Brand had a thing for theatrics, and Joe felt—he didn't have any real evidence—that what happened in Massachusetts had something to do with what happened in Texas.

He glanced across the hotel bed to the small dinner plate sitting on the sheet. The stuff on it could be the reason he was making these connections; Joe wasn't so far gone as to try and deny that. The white powder—

The cocaine, Joe.

was cut up into three neat lines, ready for his nose whenever he decided to pull the plate over. Not yet. Soon, but not yet.

No news stories connecting the events in Texas and Boston. The priest knew nothing else besides what he had told the cops. And yet, here Joe was in a three hundred dollar a night hotel room in downtown Boston, because coincidence wasn't a viable option. Brand was back. Joe didn't doubt that. Back from the dead and planning something, and then for a body to show up here, posed like Christ? No, Joe didn't believe in coincidence.

He picked up the plate and put his nose to the rolled up dollar bill he held in his hand. A quick, hard snort brought half of one line into his brain, and then he tilted his head back to make sure he got every last granule of the white dust.

What Joe did believe in was justice, but not any type that was to be levied out by the courts or even God. He believed in his own justice, and that's why he was here. His wife deserved justice. His baby, his son, deserved justice. Maybe even his father, although that was on down the list. His wife deserved justice because she had her throat slit, in front of Joe no less, due to Brand's cruelty. His son deserved justice because he'd been stolen from his crib for usage as a character in Brand's horror novel, to resurrect some long dead son.

Joe's wife, Joe's son. He was here asking questions of a priest because when he found Matthew Brand, he was going to kill him.

7

Seven

Jake took a seat in front of the desk—which looked like it didn't really want to end but did only because physics said it had to. He wore a gray suit, his tie hanging down perfectly to his belt buckle, and even with every piece of his hair placed just where it should be, he knew he was hopelessly out of his depth.

The Assistant Director of FBI Operations, Art Brayden, sat to Jake's left, and the Director of the FBI, Gyle James, sat behind the desk.

Jake was a detective for Katy, Texas—on leave now, unpaid, and there still hadn't been any discussion about how he was supposed to eat, let alone pay bills.

"How are you?" Gyle James asked, looking at Jake.

"I'm well. Thank you for having me."

"Art seems to think you have some potential to help what's happening here, so we're glad to have you aboard. Just do your best to carry your own weight, as this has already reached a point of seriousness that I doubt Texas sees much."

Jake nodded and watched Gyle turn to Art.

"We got out of the meeting with the President about an hour ago. It...well, things don't look exactly rosy. You saw the body in Boston this morning, I suppose?"

Art nodded. "In the back of the same church this time. Everything appears to be identical to the last body. The girl was murdered before she was nailed to the wood, and then taken to the cathedral. Thank God the same priest didn't find it this time. A janitor cleaning up towards the middle of the day saw it when he took out the trash."

"President's aware of it too. There's good news and then there's really bad news. The really bad news is that at least a few of the scientists pulled into that meeting see this whole thing as possible. We already have the power to split an atom. That's basically what we're talking about here, is an atom bomb. The bomb dropped on Hiroshima split an atom, which caused all the destruction. So, we've been able to do it for years, practically every developed country in the world can. What we think Brand is talking about is something like building one hundred, billion, trillion atom bombs and then launching them at the sun."

"And they think that's possible?" Jake asked, not realizing he was about to speak until the words had left his mouth. Both men looked at him.

"Some think it may be." Gyle went back to Art. "Not everyone, but probably six out of the ten in the room think Brand might be able to accomplish it. At least the part about splitting every atom in a human body. Where disagreement rises is whether he will have the ability to channel that energy and somehow fire it at the sun. Only one person said she thought it could be done, but her opinion rested on the fact that Brand was doing it. She said if anyone else attempted it, it wouldn't be possible, which doesn't really help us much."

"If he can harness the energy, but can't direct it, it'll simply blow up the world instead of the sun," Jake spoke to himself, in awe at what that meant. He had heard the call made to Art, heard Brand say the human body contained seventy trillion suns inside of it. If he tailed in taking all of that energy and hitting the sun with it, everything would explode right where he extracted it from. There would be no more world. There probably wouldn't be a sun either, because the detonation might even encapsulate objects that far off.

Both Art and Gyle were looking at Jake. "Smart, but doesn't really stay quiet, huh?" Gyle asked.

"He actually hasn't said much the whole trip over. I guess he was holding it in for this meeting."

"He's right," Gyle continued. "So we have a sixty percent chance that Brand can split all those atoms. The rest doesn't really matter. Whether or not he takes them and fires them at the sun like some kind of super missile or it blows up in his face, we're dead if that sixty percent is right."

"Jesus fucking Christ," Art said, putting a finger to each of his temples. "There's good news?"

"Kind of. As long as he's putting bodies across the city of Boston, nailing them up to crosses and what not, he's going to have a tougher time collecting the bodies he needs for all those atoms."

"That's our good news?" Art asked. "So we're not going to publish what he wants us to publish? We're not going to tell the world what's going on?"

"We're not going to tell anyone. Not our allies, not the newspapers here, no one. We're going to find Brand on our own, and until we do, let him crucify as many people as he wants. If we do anything else, if we tell anyone about this, the entire world is going to want in. The UN, China, Russia, everyone will attempt to have some kind of police force in America, all of them trying to find Brand. It'll be a cluster of cosmic proportions."

"How are we going to find him, then?"

Gyle leaned back in his chair and looked up at the ceiling. "That's the hard part, isn't it? If he keeps up this crucifixion nonsense, it'll be pretty easy to capture him. We'll simply wait for a black guy in a white van to drive into Boston, pull him out of the van, and arrest him. He's not that stupid though. No matter how much we want him to keep crucifying dead people and littering the city with them, he's going to figure out some other way to get his message out." Gyle looked down from the ceiling and over at Jake. "You got kids? Parents?"

"Parents, sir. No kids."

Gyle nodded. "Your grandkids, Art. We're going to need to get them locked down pretty hard. It would be much easier for Brand to grab up someone close to us and ransom them off for his message. I don't think the President would go for it, but it would be a better idea than the current one he's running with. Jake, you're going to want to have your parents go into hiding for a while, if you plan on staying with us. If you'd rather not work with us so that your parents don't need to go into hiding, Art and I would understand, but that's just the way this is going to be played out unfortunately."

Gyle paused, swallowed, and then continued. "Everything we have is going to be focused in Massachusetts. Everything. Every missing person that comes up, every sighting of Arthur Morgant. The scientists are making up a list of what they think Brand might need to do all this, and we're going to trace every piece of metal on that list bought in the past four years, and see what shows up in Mass. When we leave here, Art, you're going to want to have Arthur Morgant's picture on every newspaper, news program, and internet website you can think of—that's the man we're looking for, and we're looking for him because he's hanging people on crucifixes. His name isn't Arthur Morgant; it's whatever you want it to be. We don't want anyone tracing this back to The Wall and then making inferences that it's Brand. Get a team together, Art. Pull in everything we have. The scientists say there really isn't any time limit on this thing. As soon as he has fifty-five bodies, they said he can go ahead and start. He needs fifty-one more."

* * *

"I didn't want to speak in there—" Jake started.

"Really? Seemed like you did to me," Art broke in, both of them walking down the hall leading away from Gyle James' office.

"I mean, I didn't want to say anything bad about his plan. That can't really be what we're considering doing, is it? Bringing everyone in the FBI to Boston and having them, do what, look around for a black guy driving a white van?"

Art laughed. "What do you think we should do? We need people here and we need to start looking. As leads turn up, we're going to follow them and adjust our plans."

"Brand needs fifty-one bodies. That's a lot. Last time he wanted four and look at the mess he made. Fifty-one? He can't get them the same way he did last time. He's not going to be able to keep this crucifixion thing up much longer either. He has to know that. He made his point, that he's serious about us telling the world, but he won't have the time to continue this, and after this morning, he won't be able to drive an inch into Boston without someone recognizing him. The crucifixion thing is done, so what other leads are we going to be looking for?"

Art stopped and turned to Jake. "I'm not going to pull the

'how many years have you been doing this' card, but if you're going to shit on what the FBI Director just told us to do, have something better to put in its place."

"All I'm saying is, finding that many bodies is going to be hard. Especially if you're taking them from the general population. He won't be able to fly across the country and grab them one by one. He won't be able to take them from families like he did last time, because it's too many and we'll find out too fast. He's going to have to look outside of the general population, and the easiest way to do that is to take the homeless. No one misses them. No one knows they exist until they're asking for money. That's where we need to be looking. The crucifix stuff is over, and he's going to start pulling large amounts of people soon."
* * *

Art both loved and hated DC. He hated it because of the people that lived here. The vast majority of a liberal breed so pure that Art was shocked they hadn't created laws to kick out anyone who even hinted at conservative thoughts. Not that Art was a huge conservative, just that he really wasn't a fan of liberals. He lived amongst them because he had to, because his position at the FBI demanded he live in DC, and he made it a strict rule to never discuss politics with anyone within a hundred miles of the city. Once he got outside of a hundred miles, he'd begin discussing whatever was popular on the news, and his own ideology after a few drinks.

He loved DC too, though. One reason was the ability to step outside of almost any building, walk three blocks in any direction, and find a Catholic church. The good Catholics had decided to populate the nation's capital with buildings, and that was fine by Art. He had his church that he went to each week, but getting over to St. Gregory's during the middle of the day, like right now, wasn't going to happen.

Still, he needed some time to be alone with God, to think, to pray. He could always do that in his office, but interruptions happened there. Prayer wasn't as respected as much as Art would have liked, and right now, he didn't want any interruptions. He briefed Jake on who Jake would need to begin speaking with, allowed him use of his office, and told Jake that he would be back in a little bit. Art didn't mind working twenty-four hours a day if needed, as long as he could take time to pray when it struck him.

Art was glad he brought Jake to D.C. That insight into the homeless alone was something Art might not have seen. Someone else may have, and it could have risen up through the line, but not this quickly. Jake made it so that on day one, they would have the ability to watch the homeless shelters, to know who was coming up missing.

"I have blind spots. I'm old. Nearing sixty now and my blind spots are worse even than what they were four years ago," he had told Jake. "Right there, you saw one of them, and Goddamn, it was a big one. That's why you're here. No other reason. That's why I didn't say shit when you spoke up in there. You're going to get a lot of responsibility and really fast. You get to keep it as long as you don't fuck up."

The kid said okay and then Art said he was going to pray.

"You curse a lot to be going to pray."

"That's why I need to go," Art said and left Jake in his office.

He walked outside of his building into the DC heat. People in Texas didn't appreciate this heat. It might not be as hot as South Texas or Florida, but people weren't walking around in three-piece suits every day in those places. They did in DC, so the lack of temperature was more than made up for by the added clothing. Art wiped at his forehead a few feet out onto the sidewalk but kept walking.

It took him about ten minutes, but he arrived, his suit jacket draped over his arm and the back of his neck dripping sweat down into his shirt. He didn't exactly love coming out in the middle of the day to pray, but sometimes it just couldn't be avoided. Most of the time he would say something quietly at his desk, or maybe head to the john for a few minutes of silence. Today, though, none of those options would work.

He opened the door to the massive cathedral, stepping into the atrium, feeling small immediately. That's what Catholic churches did to people, and Art thought it good. The human race was nothing. All of their problems, all of their issues, all of their contrived self-importance was insignificant. The world had existed long before them and God long before that. In the end, they were all here because of God's grace, and stepping into buildings like this helped remind Art of that. He walked through the atrium and into the actual cathedral, where he dutifully formed the sign of the cross, and then walked over to a pew midway through.

The lights were dimmed as they always were at this time of the day. Art appreciated that as much as he did anything about this place, because it gave a sense of reverence and allowed him to focus easier. He bowed his head and closed his eyes, trying to find the place where he always spoke to God and sometimes God spoke back. Not often, but sometimes, if Art listened close enough.

* * *

God.

I'm scared pretty much shitless right now. Why did you create this man? I can't even begin to understand how he's running around in someone else's body. It's beyond me and yet you've put him in my way for the third time. The first time I hunted him to a cabin in the woods, the second time, to a warehouse, and now he's here again. He's here and he's threatening to destroy everything you've created.

I'm old. I'm not ready to retire exactly but I don't know if I can do this. I don't know if I can face this man down, if he's even a man. I know Jesus asked for you to take the cup from his lips, that he didn't want to drink from it. I don't want to drink from it either, Lord. I don't want anything to do with this and yet I'm not sure who else I can pass it too. There are other people in the Bureau, sure, but none that were there the last two times. I'm more scared at what failure means this time. It seems that no one is really considering that. The whole conversation with Gyle felt like we were talking about possibilities, but there wasn't any real worry that we wouldn't find him. That I wouldn't find him. And what if I don't?

Am I responsible for the death of your world?

Is that the weight which is actually being put on me right now?

* * *

Art paused, letting his thoughts sink in. He didn't open his eyes, but concentrated on whatever feeble connection he was making with God. The weight of the world was slowly descending on him in this cathedral—the realization that some seven billion people were counting on him. Were asking him, even though they didn't know it, to keep them safe. He swallowed and turned his folded hands into fists, trying to stop their shaking.

No one said those words to him in his office. No one told him, *hey, this guy who's threatening the world, he may actually be able to do the things he's claiming, and we're kind of looking at you to stop it, or we're all going to die.* No, it had been business as usual, like they were looking for some kind of bank robber.

55

Now, bearing his soul to God, Art was coming to the realization that this was no bank robber, that Brand wanted more than money. He wanted seven billion lives. Seven billion souls.

Art tried to swallow but there wasn't any saliva left in his mouth.

* * *

What the fuck am I supposed to do? Find him? Kill him? You do realize we killed him last time, right? We shot bullets through every part of his body, and he still came back. He still was able to implant his mind into someone else's.

So, what. The. Fuck. Am I supposed to do?

* * *

Art fell silent for a long time. No more angry outbursts, no more questions, just silence. Someone looking in might have thought he was sleeping, such was his stillness. Art didn't know much about meditation and he never tried to do it consciously, but when he prayed, when he felt his anger rising at a God he couldn't understand, one that didn't seem willing to make himself understandable, Art fell silent. He fell silent and listened for anything that God might give him. If nothing, fine. Art deserved nothing from God and so, while he might demand something in moments of anger, when he found his focus again, he realized that God was a being unto Himself. A being that could only be revered, not questioned.

* * *

Your will not mine. In Jesus' name, Amen.

* * *

"You're going to need to get out of town."

"Why?" Jake's mother almost shrieked over the phone. "Out of town? What the hell are you talking about?"

"Calm down, Martha. Let him talk," Pete Deschaine said.

"I can't go into detail right now. I think you'll hear about it soon enough, but you can't stay where you are. You can't go live with Aunt Belle or any of your friends from church. You need to get out of town, and I'd prefer out of the country."

Pete laughed, and Jake smiled in spite of the situation's gravity, smiled at his father's voice, laced with that supreme confidence which permeated everything he did. Thirty years in the military did that to someone. It did a lot of other things, Jake understood, but it also created a sense that one had seen everything that could be seen, so why worry any longer?

"Why do we need to leave? You got some loan sharks after you?" Pete asked.

"No. I really can't tell you, Dad. I can say though, that if you stay in the country, especially in Mississippi, much longer, you're going to be in more danger than you would be if you headed to an island for a month or something. Just think of it as a vacation. We all know that you two have the money saved up, so you could do it and not feel anything financially."

"Maybe you're right there, but I don't like being run out of my home if I don't know why," Pete said.

"How's police work in Texas got anything to do with your father and I in Mississippi?" Martha asked.

"It doesn't," Jake answered.

"Naw, it don't, Martha. What Jake's telling us here is he's either gotten in some trouble with unsavory folks or he's gotten a promotion. If it's unsavory folks, then he doesn't want us to know, and if he's gotten a promotion, then he can't tell us. That about the gist of it?" Pete asked.

"Yes, sir, that is," Jake said. His father was sir. Not every time, but a lot of the time and especially when Jake was trying to convey something important. He had said the same thing

57

when his Dad told him he wasn't to be drinking and driving after prom. "Yes, sir." He hadn't either. He had parked his car first, and then gotten about as drunk as a seventeen year old could get, throwing up all over his tuxedo but never returning to the car. Jake had built a life off his Dad believing him when he said 'yes, sir.'

He heard his Dad sigh into the phone. "Martha, you're always saying you want to visit Mexico. How long of a trip should we take do you think, Jake?"

"Three weeks for now. It might stretch out as long as two months, but I doubt that."

"Martha, we could use three weeks in the sun, and you know you'll be half drunk the whole time, so it'll feel like one week for you."

"Are you okay, Jake? Should I be worrying, because I'm going to be honest, I'm worrying pretty hard right now," his mother said.

"I'm fine, and no, don't worry. I'm just taking precautions. You're in no danger right now and most likely, if you were to stay, you would be fine. I just want to make sure."

"Okay, okay. I'll get to packing." He heard his mother hang up the phone.

"You're okay?" His Dad asked, the two of them alone on the phone now.

"Yeah. I'm fine."

"And we're going to be okay?"

"Yeah. No one even knows you exist. I imagine in a week or so you'll hear about what's going on, and then you'll think, yeah, it made sense we left," Jake said.

"Okay. We'll call from Mexico. Love you."

"Love you too."

His new boss had gone down the street to pray and Jake was alone in his office. The first call he made was to his parents, to get them out of the country. He didn't like hearing what the director had said on that subject, but the man was right. Brand wouldn't think twice about stealing Jake's parents if it meant his message might get out quicker. It was better to have them somewhere else, away from all this.

What was Art praying about? He hadn't even tried to hide it, hadn't said, "Got to deal with some personal things, be back in a few." He just said, "I'm going to pray," and then headed out of the building. Jake couldn't remember the last time he had prayed. The thought of God didn't take up much of his time, and based on Art's colorful language, Jake thought the same would hold true for him. Religious people were supposed to be pious, definitely supposed to watch their mouth.

Still, Art had left twenty minutes after receiving the most important assignment in the world, heading to a church to kneel down and ask some God in the sky for help.

The assignment.

That's what Jake would pray about if he had been one to pray.

Was this how things always worked in the FBI? Gyle James had given them almost nothing. *Go out and find Matthew Brand, use whatever you need to do it.* Jake was almost stupefied at it; how had this man risen so high in the organization? It strengthened his level of respect for Allison Moore, or at least what he knew about her. If that was the direction she'd received, she did a fine job of tracking down Brand on her own. And now Jake was here, sitting at his boss' desk with the same opportunity.

Had she been scared?

Would his father have been scared?

Jake felt fear, but not the kind he imagined Art was feeling

59

right now. He wasn't going to pray for strength or pray for wisdom. His fear rested with his father, it rested with Moore, it rested with those that came before him—and all that was to say, his fear rested within himself.

He looked down at the phone on the desk. Jake had seen one of Art's blind spots but he needed to see more. That was fine, Jake thought he would be able to find plenty of blind spots if this place kept receiving its current level of direction. The blind spots would be the easy part. He was going to pick up the phone right now, find every soup kitchen and homeless shelter in Boston, and start asking for inventory levels—if not in those exact terms. Were the homeless disappearing? If not in Boston, then Jake would spread out to other cities. If Brand was taking bodies, he wasn't doing it in public, he was doing it in the shadows, and no one lived in the shadows more than the homeless.

8

Eight

Matthew remembered sitting down at his kitchen table. A small piece of furniture in a small apartment. He was using up a lot of the cash he had stored off shore in building his new creation, but he wouldn't use an unnecessary penny for his dwelling. He had lived for ten years in an ice chamber, and now he inhabited another body, so what surrounded this body didn't matter very much to him.

He remembered sitting down for dinner though, a microwaved meal in front of him, the Salisbury steak smelling almost like steak, with only a whiff of the lab chemicals used to create his entre. He remembered picking up his fork, ready to bring the first bite to his mouth.

But now he sat in another kitchen. No fork in his hand. No plastic tray of food before him. Instead of fake Salisbury steak, he smelled cigarette smoke. Both the smell of someone currently lighting up, and also the deep, permeating smell of an area that had been smoked in for years. Matthew looked around, the kitchen he had sat down in now completely replaced. He looked at yellow tinged countertops, yellow tinged tiled floors. The sink that should have been directly in front of him lay behind him, the table he sat at was older but sturdier. A black woman was next to him, the cigarette he smelled burning in her hand. An ashtray rested beneath her cigarette so that all she needed do was flick her fingers and the ashes would fall directly to it.

"Hello?" Matthew said, unsure of anything.

"Hush yo mouth, now. I gotsta deal with something here," the black woman said without even glancing over at him. The wrinkles in her face looked like they might have been made around the time of Noah's Ark. They crisscrossed every part of her skin, looking like old road maps. Her hair was graying at the corners, but full, splaying out in a bunch of directions, untamed.

Matthew looked outside the window above the kitchen sink and he didn't recognize the neighborhood. Faded asphalt lived beneath the apartment, with two basketball goals that were missing rims sprouting up from the pavement. Another apartment complex stood directly in front of the one he was in. Matthew rose from his chair and walked to the sink, trying to get a better view of the outside world. He looked to the street, seeing cars roll slowly down tightly packed roads, cars that hadn't been in production for thirty years. There might be a few left now, but a whole road full of them? Not that many even existed anymore. Cars honked beneath him, and he tried to see their license plates, but they were too far away.

"Get in here, Arthur! Right now!" The old black lady screamed behind Matthew. He jumped, turned around, and saw that the old woman hadn't moved. She sat at the kitchen table just as calm as she had been a moment ago, despite her outburst. Matthew heard footsteps coming from somewhere in the apartment, small though, not heavy, not those of a grown man.

A little black boy walked into the kitchen. His hair was not trimmed, although not as bad as the woman at the table. Matthew knew immediately the kid was suffering from some psychological trauma, displaying symptoms from the moment he stepped into the room. He rubbed his hands against each other but didn't look down at them. His eyes stood wide open, alert, staring at the old black woman. There was fear in them, but also love. Fear and admiration. Matthew thought that this kid probably had no one else in the world. Just this old woman who might be his grandmother or his great grandmother.

"Where's your report card?" She asked.

"I gave it to you, Gramma. Gave it to you a month ago."

"You ain't give me nuttin, but you gon' give it to me. Where is it?"

The boy rubbed his hands together faster. His eyes never left his grandmother, never looked anywhere else in the kitchen. Matthew could tell the boy knew where the danger lay: the old, wrinkled woman in front of him. Nothing else in the kitchen mattered. Just what this woman decided to do.

"Gramma, I gave it to you. You looked it over. I had four B's and two A's."

"My daughter, I hope she's burning in hell right now to have pushed something out like you. You ain't given me no nothin' of a report card. Get over here," she said, flattening the butt of her cigarette into the ashtray.

Arthur walked forward. Matthew knew he didn't want to. Matthew knew the boy had some idea of what came next, and Matthew didn't think the boy was lying about the grades. Pain waited for this kid and if he had a report card he could give this old battle-axe, he would have given it to her. Instead he walked forward, hands worrying against one another.

The black woman moved with a speed Matthew found amazing. She snatched up the little boy's arms and drug him over to the kitchen sink, yelling, "Outta my way," to Matthew as she did, shoving him with a force her arms didn't seem capable of producing. She turned the knob on the faucet just as quickly as she'd wrenched the little boy from one end of the kitchen to the other.

"Now you ain't gon' lie to me no mo'. You gon' give me yo report card when I ask for it, 'cuz I ain't lettin' you turn out like yo mother or yo daddy. You understand that?"

The little boy cried, nodding, unable to pull away and unable to create an argument that would let this wild-haired lady understand that he *had* given her the report card, that she *had* looked it over.

And then the hot water touched the kid's arm, and all he could do was scream and cry.

Scream and cry.

Scream and cry.

* * *

Matthew opened his eyes.

He stared at the side of a black tray, the one he had pulled from the microwave and placed on the kitchen table. He blinked a few times, realizing he was lying face down on his table, his head turned toward his dinner. Blood pooled before him—dark, red blood. Matthew lifted himself up slowly, placing his hands on the table. Vertigo rose in his head as he pushed himself to a sitting position.

He looked down at the blood which nearly surrounded the entire tray of food. He brought his hand to his face and wiped at his nose; when he pulled away, his black skin was covered

64

with the same red liquid as the table.

What had he just seen? Who was that boy?

You know who that was. That boy was the body of the man you now inhabit. That boy, Arthur, that's the rapist's body you decided to take over when you sprang out of The Wall for the second time.

Jesus Christ.

Where had he been? New York in the 1970's? No. Detroit. Morgant was from Detroit. Somehow Matthew had relapsed back into the man's memories, experiencing life as the boy had lived it, but also inserting himself into those memories. The old woman spoke to him, actually shoved him. Morgant's mind had somehow supplanted his own, somehow risen to the top in a way much stronger than when Matthew had looked at Allison Moore's unconscious body. Morgant's mind, what was left of it, had taken over Matthew's. It hadn't made Matthew do anything besides experience that memory, but there was a hell of a lot of blood on the table that wasn't there before.

This is getting worse.

It was perhaps the most obvious and frightening statement Matthew had ever thought.

* * *

Matthew needed to think about what happened. He would have to think deep about what it meant and what he might be able to do to control it. He didn't think he could stop it, had actually thought this might happen. His mind had so severely overwhelmed Morgant's; he settled in like a Tyrannosaurus Rex might with a family of otters. The otters could do nothing but try and hide, try not to become food. Given enough time though, the otters would adapt and learn to work around the dinosaur. That's what was happening now, except the otters were also destroying the home they both shared. Their workarounds were causing synapses to misfire inside Matthew's head. Causing blood vessels to burst. Causing him to faint.

It would continue to worsen unless he found some way to slow it down. Found some way to reconnect the broken pieces. Because they were breaking, that's what was happening. His brain was breaking.

Which meant he didn't have the time he had envisioned when he dreamed this plan up four years ago. He thought that he could do this slowly, allow the world to wait in agony, searching everywhere they possibly could but unable to find him. And then, when he'd gathered his bodies, he would shut off the power source to this whole place. That was the plan, and now because of his recent daydream, things had to be expedited. He didn't have time to gather the bodies as he wanted: in slow shipments. That would need to change.

And as far as this crucifixion a day thing, his damn pride had once again created disaster in a plan that didn't need disaster. He didn't have the time to do both, to crucify women for Brayden's sake and collect the bodies for his lighthouse. He had to choose.

Matthew looked at ten crosses nailed down across his warehouse. There wasn't anything else in this place, not a single piece of wiring, not a single table. Just the wooden crosses lying across the cement. He liked Massachusetts for a few reasons. He had access to a major city, he had access to his lighthouse, and he had access to acres and acres of practically untended land. He had a busy night ahead of him. A night that would be spent in cities, not Boston—he knew he couldn't go back into Boston ever again, but there were other cities and other places to grab the women he needed. Ten would be a lot. It was audacious, actually, but his pride had gotten him into this mess and his pride would see him through it. He needed an audacious number, because the message he was sending out with these ten crosses needed to be understood. The message needed to be felt.

Ten ladies would do the trick.

* * *

The worst part about being on the road in an RV with your husband was, when you started arguing, there wasn't a whole lot that could be done. There was no going to a friend's house, no going to see a movie by yourself, no heading to a bar for a beer. You simply rode along together, not talking, until one of you decided to be the bigger person.

Karen wasn't going to be the bigger person today. Maybe tomorrow, if Martin stretched it out that long, but not today. Under no circumstances. One would think that after being married for fifty years, there wouldn't be much left to fight about. One would be wrong, if that's what one thought however. Today, Martin told her that he had changed his mind on abortion, after twenty-five years, and he no longer thought it should be legal. Told her, matter of fact, that he didn't think there was any such thing as a right to privacy, and that was just some liberal gobbledygook to kill babies that women didn't want after they bumped uglies with the wrong guy.

This information came from nowhere.

Karen. Did not. Agree.

The argument went on for about an hour. Martin continued on and on about the child's right to life, using every argument that pro-lifers had used since 1975. Nothing original, just the same old, tired arguments. She asked how he could go against the past twenty years or so of voting democrat, of actively engaging people in conversations about women's reproductive rights—of being a liberal—all in the past few months.

"Truth doesn't need time," is what he told her, and Karen could take no more. She wasn't going to sit here and listen to his nonsense the whole way up the coast. She told him to stop talking if he didn't have anything else to talk about, and so he had, and now they drove in silence.

Karen didn't mind looking out the window anyway. She'd been married to her husband long enough that she knew what he was thinking. Right now the man was sitting over there, wondering how his wife could be so dense on something that seemed so clear—without a single inclination that his complete flip-flop was incomprehensible. So, yes, she would pass on discussing anything else about abortion with him. The hills in Massachusetts weren't bad to look at either. They had traveled this road before, maybe ten times over the years, always on their trip up to Canada. They would park the RV another two hundred miles up the road, sleep for the night (they were past the point in their marriage that either one of them would ever sleep on the couch), and finish the last leg of their journey tomorrow.

"What's that?" Martin asked.

Karen didn't know if he thought she had said something or if he was asking about an object on the road, but she didn't care either way. She wasn't answering him until he either recanted the statement about abortion or at least started making sense on his new stance.

"Right there, Karen. What is that?"

He was pointing now and she followed his finger with her eyes.

Twenty feet off the road were...crosses. Ten of them in a circle, with each of the 'arms' touching the other. And...

The RV rolled closer.

People hung on the crosses.

The first thing Karen thought was that this had to be some kind of new-age art, stuff that passed for art but really wasn't even in the same genetic pool.

Martin pulled the RV to the side of the road, thirty feet away from the circle of crosses. He got out of the driver's seat without a word to her and walked along the front of the RV so that he stood on the green grass. Karen cracked her door, then opened it fully and stepped out herself.

This was no artistic enterprise. Not a single cross stood empty; naked bodies hung from each one. Different sizes, but all women, hanging nude, with blood on their faces and their hands and their feet and *oh, dear God in heaven have mercy on us sinners.*

Karen vomited on the grass, some of it spraying onto her shoes.

9

Nine

Hi, world.

My name is Matthew Brand; perhaps you remember me? Of course, there will be some newcomers to this spinning rock who were not yet born or were not yet old enough to hear about me. For them, hi! Your parents, or whoever it is you are close with, should be able to give you a brief background on me, so I need not go into it now.

Surrounding this letter are the crucified corpses of ten women. I found them all last night, nailed them all to their current homes, and then planted them all in New England soil. I had a busy night last night, and I'm tired now. Had I thought this thing out a bit more, I would have written this letter first, but if you bear with me, I think I may be able to make some progress in educating you all on my goals. This letter would have received no real traction if it wasn't combined with a dramatic display, thus the poor women who will need to be identified by their parents at morgues over the next few days. Fear not, they suffered little and were not sexually harmed. In reality, their fate is going to be much better than the people still surviving, than those reading this letter—whether that be on a newscast or the Internet, it makes no difference.

The FBI knows what I'm up to, they simply haven't made you aware of it. I've contacted them. I've told them that this would happen if they did not get my message out to you all. They refused. So, I've taken it into my hands. In a way, it's better. Now they know I'm not playing, and hopefully, you, dear citizen, know this is not a game as well. Four years ago, I killed a handful of people. Ten years before that, I killed the same number. Last night, I killed ten, and for no other purpose than to get your attention.

I trust I have it now.

The plan, what the FBI is refusing to tell you, is that within a month or two, all of you will be dead. There are Aborigines living in Australia who won't get the chance to see this letter, but they too will be dead. Everything living on this Earth, from the tiniest bacteria, to the largest mammal, all of it will die. You've all heard of the atom bomb, doubtlessly remember the devastation it caused in Japan last century. I've found a way to create about one hundred billion, trillion of those—and that's on the conservative side, really. You see, each one of you, each human being on this Earth has countless atoms inside themselves. If we could part one human from the energy inside his or her atoms, we could power cities for years and years. I know how to do it. I'm including, with this note, a copy of the formulas I derived to accomplish it, with a few key parts redacted. No need to give the governments of this oppressive planet any more firepower, as I'm sure you agree. The point here is that I have the knowledge, as well as the capability, to harvest energy from human beings.

Why would I want to do that? Am I planning on stopping climate change? Ridding the world of fossil fuels? Ah, but then remember the paragraph above where I said I would kill you all?

I'm going to use the energy I extract from fifty-five humans (to be honest, I picked that number because that's all I could fit on the contraption I built to hold all of this energy) and fire it at our sun. That life giving orb that we take for granted every single day, the

71

thing that allows the flowers to bloom and your babies to thrive. So what happens when I hit it with one hundred trillion suns of my own? I have two theories, but I lean (and hope) to the second. The first is that all of that energy in one place, at one time, causes the sun to contract massively and in the shortest of time you can imagine, before bursting out in a supernova. That would mean we all die by fire about seven minutes later. I hope that doesn't happen. I really do. The second option, and what I think is most likely—though these things are never definite in cosmology—is that the sun simply dies. All of the gasses in the ball are burnt up within a day or so, and nothing is left but a hardened rock.

Then comes the fun part.

For the next month, you wait it out. You hope that scientists can somehow figure out a way to live without the sun, and believe me, they'll be working furiously. They won't succeed, however. The atmosphere will hold in much of the heat that the Earth currently has, but everything else stops. Plants die in a few days. Animals are blinded and die from thirst or starvation. Disease breaks out en masse across humanity as they now lack the vitamin D needed to fight off infection. Within a month, everyone's dead.

That's what I'm bringing to all of you.

The world didn't want me to have my son. They thought it terrible that I wanted the cops who shot him, who filled his young body with bullets, to pay with their lives so that he could have his again. I wasn't asking for a lot. Justice. Maybe for some of you to look the other way while a father went and dealt with the people who had harmed his family. Four years ago, Allison Moore (who is one of the first four in my Death to the Sun plans, followed by her daughter, and the literary giant Jeffrey Dillan/his girlfriend) decided that maybe I shouldn't have my wife either. She decided that my wife might be a good idea to take from me, and so she did, first mentally, and then physically.

This world left me with nothing but my mind. You celebrated my achievements when I was formulating genetic theories that halted aging. You celebrated my accomplishment when I created the first viable treatment for cancer that didn't cause the destruction of healthy cells in the human body. When I gave to you, you celebrated, but when I asked for you to give back to me, you refused. You took everything I had and left me with nothing.

So, world, this will be my gift to you. I will take everything. I will take your sons, your daughters, your family, your futures. All of it belongs to me now, and I'm going to cast it all into eternal darkness, where nothing will ever rise again.

Cheers, friends.

Matthew Brand, Ph.D.
* * *

"You better have more for me than what you had yesterday. A lot more."

Gyle paced behind his desk. His hands were in his pockets, his eyes looking at the floor, his mouth barely opening as he spoke. There wasn't anger in his voice, just resolution—at what, Art didn't really know. He had known Gyle for ten years, but never heard this voice before.

"Well, we have something. I don't know if it's what you would term a lot, though."

"You've both seen the news over the past eight hours, right? You've both seen the immaculate handwriting of Matthew Brand—whom the experts have identified as a one hundred percent match, by the way—plastered all over the television? They're looking at his formulas right now and all I've heard is that it's mind blowing. I'm not sure what it takes to blow the minds of astrophysicists, but I imagine it's quite a lot. So, please, Art, or your wonder boy here, tell me what you've done in the past day."

Art sat down on the chair in front of his desk. Jake remained at the door, hands behind his back. Gyle kept pacing.

"Jake had probably the best idea out of anyone yesterday, and we're searching deeper into it right now. I'm not sure if last night's little soiree will cast doubt on Jake's theory, but he doesn't think Matthew is going to play the game the way he played it last time. He doesn't think Brand is going to try to find people that are attached to families. It's too dangerous, especially for the amount of people he's trying to take. Even last night, he barely pulled off the crucifix stunt. By one in the morning, people were reporting these women missing. Male dates were heading to cop stations, talking about some black assailant having taken their girlfriends. Had he hung out another hour, there wouldn't be anything to discuss this morning except how quickly we could have Brand strapped into the electric chair. So, I think Jake's right. He can't go after people this way because of the sheer number, fifty-one now, that he's trying to grab. He would make a mistake. Someone would see him. He wouldn't be able to kill every witness. We would pin him down. There's just too many variables he couldn't control. Jake pointed all that out and then asked who could he take? Who could be snapped up and no one ever notice? The homeless. We're already looking at shelters and soup kitchens across Mass and New England, and we're stretching that out to all of the northern states today as well, looking for abnormal disappearance rates, looking for drops in clientele at homeless shelters, et cetera." Art folded his hands on his lap and crossed one leg.

Gyle stopped pacing, but didn't turn to face anyone.

"What have you found?" He asked.

"Nothing," Jake said from behind Art. "No one has seen anything abnormal."

"So he had this great idea, and as of now, it's panned out to exactly nothing."

"It's only been a little over twenty-four hours, Gyle."

"I have another meeting with the President today. World leaders are calling. The President of Russia has been on the phone with our President for an hour, trying to figure out if this is a hoax. We need more from you, Art, and if you're staying, Deschaine, we need more from you as well."

Art nodded while Jake only looked on.

"The pressure has picked up. Yesterday, we could go about this the way we wanted because we had time. Today, there's no time. Today, we should have had Brand captured yesterday. Today, I need more. So tell me, now, what's the plan for today, for tomorrow, for this week. What overarching plan do you have to stop the destruction of the world?"

Art looked out the window behind Gyle. He had never wanted to sit in this office. He had never wanted to be a phone call away from the President's voice. Gyle had. Gyle wanted to push himself so high and so far that he might one day sit in the White House himself. One wanted it and one didn't. One had it and one did not. Yet, here were both of them in the exact same situation—Art almost able to feel the President's breath on his own neck.

"Are you worried about the President, Gyle? Be honest with me. Is that what this is?"

Gyle's head snapped up as quickly as a dog's mouth clamps down on food. Art knew Gyle rose this high because he could play politics, and that meant he wouldn't let someone slander his character. Hard work and hard networking all came into play this high up and here was a direct report questioning his character.

"You want to ask me that question again, Art?"

"I mean, what are you really worried about? Do you think Brand's going to be able to do what he says he will? Is that what is scaring you? Or is it the fact that we might look like fools again?" It hadn't been easy on Gyle four years ago. He had been in Art's current position, and the field operations looked like bumbling idiots as Brand pranced around the country increasing his body count. Somehow Gyle had survived the purge, even moving up.

"Step outside for a second, please, Deschaine." Gyle didn't look away from Art as he spoke.

The door closed leaving the two of them alone.

"If you ask me something like that in front of a subordinate again, you're fired. Do you understand that?" Gyle asked.

Art nodded. "I do. I'm sorry."

"No. I don't think this guy can blot out the sun. I don't care what those scientists think; it's a farce. He's insane. He's always been insane. Maybe twenty-five years ago he was some kind of genius making massive changes in the world, but that's all in the past. Twenty-five years before that people were using rotary phones and no women worked outside of the home. Twenty-five years is a long time, Art, and whatever this guy used to have is gone. It's been replaced by some freak of nature, rapist monster walking around acting like he's still the same man from all those years ago. He's not. He's nothing like that man. I don't know if these scientists are having their collective minds blown like they're being visited by a Vegas prostitute because they think he's the same man, or what, but

76

no. Categorically no, I do not think he can do what he's claiming. And that leads me to yes, it is the President that is bothering me. It's the international pressure that's now being put on this whole event which is causing me to lose it. I don't want to look like we did four years ago. I won't look like we did four years ago. If you're going to turn into another Allison Moore, then I'll go ahead and take your resignation now. If you think you can handle what I'm asking, then I want a strategic report on my desk by midnight tonight."

   * * *

Joe Welch held the letter in his hand. He had printed it off a hotel computer earlier this morning.

Joe traced his fingers over the lettering. The man's handwriting truly was beautiful, awesomely so. Joe even liked the way Brand constructed prose. Every word both flippant and of all importance. He had read it a hundred times, at least, and thought that he might read it a hundred more before the evening was over. He printed the thing off around nine in the morning, had a single egg for breakfast, and then came back up to his bedroom to sleep. It was the first time in forty-eight hours he had closed his eyes outside of blinking. Joe was no longer in Boston, but had followed the crucifixes out to the small New England town of Licent. He found a bed and breakfast, swiped his credit card, and then went directly to the site where the crucifixes were found.

Just a day after ten dead girls were posted on crosses, it all was cleaned up. The only things left in the field were the holes left from the wood. Joe was close to Brand but needed to be closer. He didn't know how to get there yet.

It didn't trouble him though, that he didn't know exactly what he was going to do. This wasn't an *if* thing for Joe, it was a *when*.

A year after Patricia's death, his mindset changed from if to when. He decided the direction the rest of his life would take and forsook everything outside of that direction.

He had lived with his brother for a year, the year after Patricia's death, the year after his son, Jason, turned into a science experiment with holes poked into his body. Joe hadn't started using cocaine yet, instead he lived in his brother's basement—his life nothing but darkness and television reruns. His brother's wife might have had some problems with him being there, but either she kept her mouth closed or Larry kept her misgivings from Joe. She couldn't understand, and really, neither could Larry. Larry wasn't exactly a brother, not if the DNA and bloodline were to be consulted; he was a distant cousin that had come to live with Joe and his mother a couple years after Brand killed Joe's father. Maybe Brand knew about him, maybe he didn't, but he had left Larry alone, so neither he nor his wife could know the terror that Joe had lived with much of his life or the sorrow he lived with now. That first year had been dark. Comparatively, the cocaine and rushing around the country for evidence was a tiny piece of heaven.

Joe watched a lot of television, if watching meant lying in bed while images streamed over his eyes. The screen was small, little bigger than a computer monitor, and he watched sitcoms. Every one that seemingly existed, both in and out of production. He knew every character's name; he knew their back stories; he had predictions on where the show would take them. It became, or rather the people in the shows became, his family. The brother and sister-in-law that lived upstairs were roommates. People he saw from time to time if he decided to join them for dinner, which was a rare, rare thing.

Dinner, during that first year, had been awkward at best.

78

Joe didn't know what to say to these people. He didn't know what they wanted to talk about and he knew he didn't have a single topic worthy of discussion. If they wanted to talk sitcoms, he might be able to add some value, but other than that, what did he have? He could talk about feelings. They tried that the first few times, Larry asking how Joe *felt*.

Joe told him, and the dinner ended with Joe's plate on the floor, tears streaming down his and Larry's wife's face with the vast majority of the meal going uneaten. So they quit talking about feelings when Joe came to dinner and tried to move onto other things. Eventually, Larry and Sara-Beth spoke as Joe ate in silence. Which was fine with him. The awkwardness abated some, and he needn't wait until they were finished eating before he cleared his plate and headed back down to the basement.

He couldn't sleep back then, which turned out to be ironic, because that's all he wanted to do now. Besides find Brand. That took precedence, of course.

The first year, he tried to sleep, but he only saw Patricia when he closed his eyes. He saw her in front of him again. Her eyes wide, sweat blossoming across her forehead and upper lip. Pain lit through her eyes, pain and fear. Then the knife came down. Joe knew it would come, knew it each time he dreamed of her, that the knife was going to drop and she couldn't escape it even if he begged the knife to stop. The knife came down, began separating flesh directly under Patricia's left ear, and had it been only that one poke, maybe everything would have ended fine. Instead, the knife pulled across her throat, opening it as if it was a Ziploc bag. Blood poured out like it had simply been waiting for someone to give it the go-ahead, like it actually *wanted* out of his wife's body. The blood was a traitor.

That's what he saw every time he tried to sleep and so he

finally stopped trying. Even if he did fall asleep, he woke up soon after, as soon as that blood started to drop. It occurred to him at this point that he may need to develop a drug habit. He didn't get his brother's permission, didn't mention it to them despite living in their house. He paid his rent and he didn't cause trouble. During that first year he sold his landscaping business for a nice sum, given that he had contracts locked up on multiple business parks for the next four years. He didn't spend money, besides his rent and his portion of the utilities, so he could afford to develop the habit, and he needed one because he needed to not see his wife dying nightly.

The question was, what habit to develop? He tried drinking, which put him to sleep, but did nothing to squelch the dreams. They still came, only now he couldn't wake up because of the drunken stupor he created inside himself. So alcohol was out. The next two logical choices were heroin or cocaine. He tried cocaine first because needles just seemed a bit too far, which was kind of funny when he thought about it: searching for an addiction, but would rather avoid needles if possible-- it sounded like some kind of Craigslist ad. He would have gone to heroin, without a doubt, had the cocaine not done the job. Maybe had he tried heroin first, he wouldn't be sitting in this small town, searching for a man who looked completely different than the one that killed his wife. Maybe he would have overdosed in Larry's basement, and maybe that would have been for the best.

Alas, it turned out he liked cocaine.

Dopamine and serotonin filled his brain in a way he didn't know possible. The sadness of his loss was immediately replaced by the happiness of the time he had been able to spend with both his wife and son. Even watching her sit tied up while her throat was slit paled some, unable to reach the full crescendo of pain that he felt when sober. There wasn't anything else he could do to match the feeling and he realized he had found his habit. He didn't want to go back to the darkness of the room, go back to the constant and pervasive thoughts of his lost family.

So Joe picked up an addiction, and decided to figure out what he would do with the rest of his life.

Looking at the letter, fresh up from his nap and no cocaine ingested yet, Joe wondered if Brand knew he was coming for him. Probably not, and if he did, he wouldn't care. Brand thought himself invincible. The letter showed that, if nothing else. The man thought the world was created for him, and because it didn't give him exactly what he wanted, it had somehow betrayed him. So he would punish the world, and in his mind, what could one man do against him? Nothing. Joe hoped Brand was thinking like that; it would leave him vulnerable. It left him only looking for the big things, not the small ones, and he would make mistakes then. Small ones, but mistakes.

Joe understood that the FBI was hunting Brand too, but Joe and the FBI had very different ideas of what should happen once someone found him. Joe made his decision, the decision of what he would do if he found Brand, early on. The FBI had failed to truly avenge his father's death, his wife's death, his son's death. Each time they tried, somehow, improbably, impossibly even, Brand came out on top. Joe decided that he wouldn't allow that to happen again. That if the FBI was incapable or unwilling to kill Matthew Brand, as they seemed to be, then he would do the job himself. He would kill Brand and there needn't be any law enforcement involvement for that to happen—indeed, Joe preferred they stay out of his way.

10

Ten

It had taken Matthew three years to make this drive.

Three years ago Matthew began putting out feelers, searching for what he thought might be the best way to quietly amass the number of people he would need. He thought about the homeless, that had been his first thought actually—but it was too risky. People looked for the homeless, even if they looked less than for almost any other demographic. They still looked. If twenty people came up missing in New York City, twenty people that had inhabited the same spot for years, the FBI might hear about it. Too risky. He couldn't have risk now. Risk had gotten him to this point. Risk had gotten his son killed again and his wife killed for the first time. Risk, and Matthew's own damnable pride, had put him in this position and he wouldn't allow those two things to rise again.

So he thought and he searched for six months. He came to a conclusion right before he showed up and gave Dillan what was owed him.

There was one group that people didn't look for at all. One group that even parents, if they were around, would disown.

Prostitutes.

They were the scourge of society. The women that threw away one of the most sacred of civilization's morals: that women shouldn't sleep around. More, they shouldn't be paid to sleep around. Parents raised children, especially girls, with that specifically in mind. Keep your legs closed until you find a man who loves you. So the ones that opened their legs for a few dollars, *oh, Lord, they couldn't be forgiven.*

Matthew's thought process didn't end there though. He couldn't start pulling call-girls off the street; their absence would be recognized perhaps quicker than the homeless. What he needed was the sex trade. He needed people that were so lost, so drugged up, so completely forgotten that they could barely remember their own names, let alone someone writing it down in a police precinct somewhere.

Today, three years later, with four bodies hanging in his lighthouse, Matthew arrived at one of the three men who ran the sex trade in North America. He parked his van outside of a building, the parking lot full of cars, and a sign at the top of the building, which said *StraightAire*—a business name that Matthew had found out wasn't just a front. They had legitimate revenues and the cars here weren't just for show. People worked inside the building, even if it was conveniently set off from the main highway by about five hundred feet of road and a security guard. Matthew didn't ask questions when he was told to arrive though, didn't ask how they were going to get the people he needed into his van and didn't ask what the people working at *StraightAire* would think if they happened to witness someone dressed in rags being shoveled into a van.

He only showed up, because this was a business you didn't ask questions in, and this was his first time meeting any of these people in person. Plus, he was already going to ask something outrageous, and he needed to save whatever small amount of political capital he might have. When he first came up with this plan, low risk was all-important. Time was not a factor because as long as he gathered the people he needed, he could dim the sun at any time. That theory had changed this past week, had changed drastically when Matthew woke up with blood covering much of his kitchen table and a distinct memory of having being shoved by a black woman who no longer existed. Something was taking place in his mind, and he didn't know what the end result would be. He couldn't control it. Matthew had only felt that way once before, felt that he had no control over his life when he watched those four cops go to trial for Hilman's murder. He sat in the courtroom every day, right next to Rally, holding her hand, and listening as they lied repeatedly.

He was behaving aggressively.

He was cursing.

He was using racial epithets and making threats.

It had gone on and on, and the prosecutor seemed to care, but seemed to be fighting a machine that would just as soon eat him as let him live. Matthew felt helpless the day they read the verdict of not-guilty. He felt like a newborn, with strange light filling up his vision, now in a new world that he didn't understand. He wouldn't feel that way again, though, not until now.

This week, when he woke up from that daydream, he felt comparable to the way he had in the courtroom. Not as deeply, but a vague similarity that this was something outside of his sphere of influence. So what could he influence? The speed at which he operated. Or at least, he could try to, which is what he wanted to ask these people today. *Would it be possible to turn the assembly line's pace up just a bit?*

Matthew stepped outside of the van and closed the door. He walked to the hood, just as he had been instructed to, and placed a cigarette in his mouth, just as he had been instructed to. He lit it and smoked. He tried smoking in college but this was the first one he had lit since then. It felt, strangely, good. He blew the smoke out into the sky and took another puff. He was told to wait here until someone came for him. Matthew didn't think that someone would be a law enforcement agent; he had done as much investigating as humanly possible on the people he was dealing with, as surely they had him. Maybe they knew who he really was, or maybe they believed the spurious life he had created and allowed to circulate through the various regulatory agencies. He'd even popped in some contacts to cover up the blue of his eyes, making them the more natural brown of African-Americans. Either way, he was here, and you didn't get here unless they thought you were serious. No one arrived to this business and ended up dead right away. You got here because you had money to give and they had people to sell.

The door to *StraightAire* opened up and a man walked outside. He had a blazer on, a button down shirt with the top two buttons left unbuttoned. No tie. He walked across the parking lot, his eyes looking more at the ground than anything else, certainly not sweeping the lot.

"Jamal?" The man asked as he arrived.

"Yes, sir. Mr. Bolden?"

"That would be me. How was the drive?"

"Not bad at all. Eighteen hours is never good, but it wasn't bad either," Matthew said.

"Good, good. The drives can really be the worst sometimes. If you need a pick-me-up for the drive home, let me know and we can probably find you something."

"I should be okay, but I appreciate it."

The man nodded. "Alright, let's get to it." He turned and started walking back across the parking lot. Matthew dropped the cigarette and followed.

They went through the building, winding upwards, taking the stairs each time, and covering each floor. The floors were full of people in cubicles, apparently working, as if nothing out of the ordinary was going on. And, really, nothing abnormal *was* happening yet, but why was Matthew being led upstairs? Upstairs meant they had to come back down, and back down meant they had to travel in front of all these people again. Matthew kept his mouth shut until they reached the top floor, where they walked all the way to the end and met what appeared to be a closet.

"Here we are," Mr. Bolden said.

He didn't put a key into the doorknob, but simply turned it, and opened the door. The room was dark, but as he flipped a switch, the ceiling rained down light. They both stepped in, and Mr. Bolden closed the door behind them, though anyone could have looked in to see what this room held.

The Room of Illegitimacy, Matthew thought.

Four people were attached against a wall. Their legs tied to pipes that ran around the base, and their arms to pipes that ran at about waist level. Two sets of pipes, four people attached to them with zip-ties.

Matthew turned around to look at Bolden. "Those people out there, the one's you just paraded me through, they know?"

"Of course. They're paid their usual salary, and then they receive a bonus once a year just like any other corporation. Their bonus is tied to their performance and tied to their knowledge of this room."

"And if someone leaves the company?" Matthew asked.

"Once you work for StraightAire, you receive your bonus for the rest of your life. If at any time you feel the bonus isn't enough, then an unfortunate accident may occur. Trust me, Jamal, we vetted you, we vetted these people, too. You can guess why I walked you through the way I did rather than simply taking an elevator."

"It's a smooth operation," Matthew said, before turning around to look at his purchases. All four were Asians. One boy, three women. The boy was just that, a boy. He might have been fourteen, probably having started puberty, but not very far into it. The three women were young, eighteen tops. One had a bruised eye and Matthew walked over to her. He had to look down just a bit so that he could see her face. She didn't look up.

Matthew saw nothing in those black, slightly slanted eyes. A blankness comparable to what he had seen in Marley Moore.

"Sometimes accidents happen, but it's only a bruise. It will heal in a day or so," Bolden said from behind him. Matthew realized Bolden thought he was looking at the girl like he was checking inventory. Matthew was looking because he had never seen a sex slave before. He was looking because he wanted to try and understand perhaps a sliver of what these people went through. Not out of compassion, but out of that singular curiosity that drove him so far in life. The curiosity to ask why. To continually ask why. There weren't any answers in the girl's eyes though. No answers to her past or her current mind.

"There's a problem," Matthew said, still staring at the girl.

"And what's that?"

"These aren't enough."

Matthew turned around and saw that Mr. Bolden held a gun,

as if it had dropped from the ceiling and landed in his hand with the silence of a butterfly.

"I don't like problems, Jamal."

"Neither do I, but you don't need that gun to solve this one. I need more people is all. I'll pay. I'll pay a premium above what I'm already paying because I realize it's going to put more pressure on your operation." Matthew's hands hung at his sides, the rest of him not moving at all.

Bolden's gun faced the floor, but Matthew saw his finger wrapped around the trigger. "This is my first time meeting you. We had a deal. Four people for a certain amount of money. We have your money, you have your people, but you show up now and say that you want to change the deal. You're saying that you want more. How many more, Jamal?"

"As many as you can get at once. Twenty, maybe."

"You want twenty people at once, as opposed to the four we agreed on. How do you think that looks to me?"

Matthew said nothing.

"It looks suspicious, like maybe you're wanting me to find more people because you're wanting to build a stronger case against me. Like maybe a life sentence wouldn't be enough for you and your friends."

Matthew laughed loud and heavy. "I see. I see. I'm going to turn around here, if you don't mind, and look back at the merchandise for a second. Try not to let the gun fire into my back if you can." He turned and stepped closer to the girl. "Mr. Bolden, I can promise, I'm not interested in either a life sentence or a death sentence for you."

In an instant, Matthew brought a blade from his pocket and opened the girl's throat. He stepped back quickly to avoid being splashed too much, and her life flooded to the floor. He hadn't escaped all of it though, some having sprayed immediately onto his white shirt and face. He didn't move to wipe any of it off.

He turned around and looked at the man holding the gun. Turning his palms towards Bolden, the blade still in his right hand, the girl hanging limply behind him, Matthew said, "I'm not too interested in getting the authorities involved at all."

* * *

Art heard his phone ringing and turned on his side to look at it. He was in his office, lying on a couch against the wall. Jake was outside, sleeping on the floor with his undershirt as a pillow. Both men had flights so early in the morning it would make a dairy farmer embarrassed at the time he woke up, so the two decided to stay here, work until they couldn't any longer, and then leave from the office. Art's phone said it was two in the morning and they would be waking up in the next thirty minutes anyway. He picked the phone up, still ringing with an unknown number, and put it to his ear.

"Hello," he said and then cleared his throat.

"Art! Matthew! Did I catch you sleeping?"

The voice sounded entirely too happy to be up this early. Art thought, haphazardly, but thought nonetheless, about what they had done with his phone. He told IT the last time Brand called and they put a tracer on it, so Art didn't need to worry about that.

"Was just waking. How can I help you?" Art said, sitting up on the couch.

"Just calling to check in. Got some really good news today from one of my partners, wanted to see how things were going on your end. Splendidly, I hope?"

Art leaned forward to look out his office door, and saw Jake sprawled on his stomach, the t-shirt forgotten to the right of

89

his head.

"If sleeping in my office is splendid, then yes, you would be correct. What the fuck are you calling me for?"

"Art, you do realize I'm going to be like the closest person you have in this world over the next couple of months, right? That you're going to die knowing me better than you know perhaps anyone else. You don't have a wife. You see your kids and grandkids twice a year. You have your job and I think you have a little sidekick now, but that's it. No one else. So why are you upset that I'm calling you?"

Art stood up, stretched one arm above his head, and looked for his computer bag. "You like having a bigger dick now that you're black?" He walked across the room for the bag, and threw a laptop inside it. He would need to wake up Jake in a few minutes.

"To be honest, haven't been able to use it very much. Maybe someday soon though. This Arthur Morgant character, he's tougher than I imagined. Might have decided to dive into the other guy at The Wall had I known all the baggage this one would bring."

Art stopped packing.

Use it soon? "Morgant was a rapist," Art said.

"Yeah, I know." Brand sighed. "It seems that all of those tendencies cannot be simply shoved aside forever. Don't worry though, I haven't resorted to his more base ways yet. I'm still fighting the good fight, you know?"

Art laughed quietly into the phone. "You're a sick fuck. You're going to end all life on the world and become a rapist at the same time, in the last year of your life. That's what all your genius has led you to."

"Come on, don't say it like that. It sounds so, I don't know, depressing. I'll give it to you though, I'm certainly not peaking in my late age, which is why my partner's agreement today is really such good news. I don't want this to be my Canterbury Tales, you know?"

"Agreed. I'd hate for you to die in some hole or get caught raping some woman at a Seven-Eleven. That would take away a lot of the pleasure I plan on having at your next death. The Wall's no more. The whole program scrapped. There's nowhere else for that big brain of yours to hide after we put a few holes through it."

Matthew laughed then. "Are God fearing men supposed to be filled with so much hate?"

"Probably not, but God made confession for a reason."

"That he did. Maybe that's what you are to me, Art. Maybe you're my confession over the next few months."

Art took his phone away from his face and looked at it, letting the silence stretch between the two of them. Art was going to act as a priest to this man, was going to listen to his sins, was going to try and help absolve him? He put the phone back to his ear. "I'm not sure you understand what confession is."

"I'm not asking for absolution. I'm not asking for anything, but you will get these calls, Art. You will get them, and protocol is going to determine that you have to listen to them, because I might drop a hint of what's going on, of a way that you can stop me." Matthew paused for a few seconds. "Haven't been able to find anything on me yet, huh?"

They were flying to Massachusetts this morning, a team had already been assembled including police forces. They were hitting every industrial park in the state. It might not be the best path, but where else could they start? He was in the state of Mass, that much was clear, and last time he had used the industrial park. So with warrants from every needed judge, they were going to make sure he wasn't doing it again. That was it though. The homeless situation wasn't panning out. Any and all missing persons reported were to be immediately entered into the FBI database, to which analysts were pouring over the data as it came in from across the country. So far, nothing substantial had come back.

"My boss, he doesn't believe you can do it."

"Do you?"

"No. You lost your mind a long time ago, Brand. Your best work was done before that. Even the technology that allowed you to bring your son back, that was done twenty years ago. You've done nothing since then that would even hint at you having this kind of power anymore."

"Besides create an exact replica of my mind and insert it over someone else's?"

"Which, apparently, is breaking down on you right now." Art looked up to see Jake at the door. He took the phone away, hit the speaker button, and laid it on the desk.

"Has Jake joined us? Is that why I hear a slight echo?" Matthew asked.

"We're both here, but we're going to have to cut this short pretty soon. Gotta catch a flight to come to where you are. Anything you want to say to us before we get off?"

The phone was quiet for a few seconds.

"I can't think of anything super important right now. I'll call back if something comes up. You two take care. Bye now."

The screen read call ended, leaving Art and Jake alone in the dark room.

"How long had that been going on?" Jake asked.

"I don't know, five minutes maybe. The call woke me up."

"You sounded awfully friendly with him."

"Would you rather I had cussed him?" Art asked. "It doesn't matter. He seems to think he's going to keep calling back and we're going to continue to have these little chats. The whole thing was recorded, probably being uploaded by my phone right now. Get a listen to it either on the plane or when we land. Something's not right with him though." Art sat down on the couch and started tying his shoes.

"What do you mean?"

"Not like the obvious 'he's a fucked up individual something's not right with him', but something is going wrong internally. He told me he was getting urges to rape. Flat out said it. You know anything about Arthur Morgant, the body he's in?"

"He was abused heavily by his grandmother as a child. That's one reason he didn't get the death penalty. He graduated high school, worked for a fast food chain, and started raping women probably around the age of fifteen."

Art looked up, a shoelace in each hand. "You got more?"

"Yeah. I just didn't know if you wanted me to drone on about him."

"No, that's fine. More than fine really." Art shook his head and went back to tying his second shoe. "He said that Morgant's base instincts were bubbling up, and I don't know what that means, but we need to run it by some of the medical guys. It sounds like he's got some urges that aren't indigenous to his own mind, and that could lead to him making some pretty serious mistakes."

"Like raping women," Jake said, putting his t-shirt back on his thin frame.

"Like raping women," Art agreed.

* * *

It took Jake an hour to drive to the site where Brand left his

93

letter. He drove it alone, telling Art he wanted to see the spot and wanted some time to think.

"You're serious?"

"You pray alone; I think alone."

Art let him go. It was an hour outside of Boston, where the operation was being housed.

He pulled his car to the side of road, got out, and walked to where the long wooden poles had been dug into the ground. The mayor of this little town had made sure they were pulled out as soon as humanly possible, not wanting anyone else to see such a horrible sight, probably. Jake had studied the pictures repeatedly over the past few days, looking at the coroner's report, looking at both the lumber and the autopsy photos. Each one of the women died the same way, a puncture wound to their brain. All of the crosses were precisely the same. Same height. Same weight. Same dimensions. As far as Jake could tell, it looked like they had actually rolled off a Ford assembly line the same as a car would.

He looked down into one of the holes. It was deep, a good foot down. Brand had been out here in the early morning digging ten of these, then dragging everything out and planting them deep so that they wouldn't shake. Jake didn't know if he could accomplish that if given a week. Brand had done it in a night.

Jake's father told him once about a soldier in one of his platoons. Pete said the guy wouldn't back down to anyone. He would take orders, but if at any point he thought someone was getting lippy, the guy would just start punching. Didn't matter if they were generals or private first class, if he felt insulted he was going to fight. Jake's Dad said he admired the kid, in a way, but thought he was awesomely dumb as well. It was like he had to prove himself to every single thing on this planet.

If a fern could somehow insult the guy, he would rip the fern out of the ground and burn it. He was set on letting the world know that he mattered, that no one could take that away from him. Except, his Dad said, they already had. They took it away from him the moment he decided to fight, because then he had already decided the world's opinion mattered.

Jake was beginning to feel like that guy now. He wouldn't call his pops and tell him, but he kept thinking back to Moore. Even now, walking around this grassy lawn, he was wondering what she would have seen here. The woman went right to the edge with Brand, pushing past limits that no one knew existed, and even though she lost, she won too. She went further than anyone dreamed against the smartest man to ever live. Now here Jake was, walking around by himself in this field, and faced with a very similar predicament.

You know, no one cares, right? His father said. Or, the voice that Jake created for his father.

It was completely true. If he brought this up to Art, this insecurity about his own contributions versus Moore's, he'd be laughed at and possibly kicked off the case, sent back to Texas to work on local convenience store robberies. If he told it to his father, his father might listen, but in the end what did comparing yourself to a dead woman matter to a man that had most likely shot people in half with machine guns? No, no one else but him cared at all. What they cared about was stopping this man. They cared about killing a heinous criminal.

And Jake was here, looking into an empty hole, and comparing himself to Moore.

And what exactly is wrong with that? What's wrong with wanting glory, with wanting to go up against the best?

In his mind, nothing. As long as he did his job, did it matter the reason he did it? As long as he did his best to find Brand, what did it matter if it was for his own glory or to stop a crime? The results would be the same.

The wooden crosses flashed through his mind with a speed that stopped all his self-analysis.

The wooden crosses.

The wood.

All of it was the exact same. Forty logs that were all cut the same, that all weighed the same.

Brand had to gather them all from the same spot. He didn't go looking around for forty different logs at forty different stores. He bought them all from one place. How many people could have bought those exact dimensions in that exact quantity?

Don't get half-cocked yet. He could have bought a massive quantity.

All the better. Easier to find.

And what if he bought a lot of lumber, all of it different sizes, and he pulled out those select pieces to make the crosses?

That was a definite possibility, but still, was anyone looking into this yet? He needed to find out.

He gazed out across the field once more, trying to forget his own internal drama, trying to forget his own drive. A lot of women had died and then been dragged out here, naked, thrown up on boards like the dolls of wicked children.

Try to remember them. At least some of the time.

11

Eleven

My name is John Randolph and welcome to *Nightline.*

Tonight we're going to show you the aftermath of Matthew Brand's letter. The police, the FBI, and even the CIA are filing out across the nation, searching for the man who says he holds the key to the entire world's salvation. A man who says that we will never see the key again, that he has no intention of saving the world, instead he's going to throw it into eternal darkness. Matthew Brand's letter shook America, and even the world, to its core. Tonight we're going to show you images of the aftermath. Some of this will be shocking. Some of it will be heartwarming. If you have young children watching you may want to put them to bed. We're going to show you a piece of America, a piece of the world, that many of you might not have known existed.

This is the small town of Licent where the ten crucified bodies were found. Ten women, all in a circle, found by an elderly couple making a yearly cross-country drive. The town is peaceful, even four days later. People are going to work like normal. People are acting, generally, as if one of the most horrific scenes in America's criminal history had not just played out on their soil.

I had the opportunity to speak with a store clerk at Wal-Mart, the first and only national chain in the entire town.

"Why are things so calm here?"

"I, uh, well I've been here my whole life. I went to high school here. I'm even taking some classes at the community college here. This town, I guess it doesn't spook easy. I mean, we've seen the news, watched what's happening in other places, and I think we would just be embarrassed if that turned out to be us, you know? I was talking with my parents about this last night, they live here too, and my Dad just said, 'well, we all die', and I really think that's how much of the town feels. No one else has said it, but I think we're just kind of looking at this man, this Matthew Brand, as another possible way we could die. We're not going to lose our minds about it though. There's some good law enforcement after him, and they've caught him before, so they'll do it again. We're just not going to lose our minds."

I heard that general sentiment echoed throughout my time in Licent.

The next city I went to was Atlanta, Georgia. I wanted to pick a major city, somewhere that people knew, and somewhere that could be representative of other large cities across the nation.

What you're looking at right now is downtown Atlanta. The street is Peachtree Street North West, and what's in front of you is a liquor store known as Green's. There were bars on the windows yesterday, and now you can see them discarded amongst the broken glass across the parking lot. The store clerk, thank God, managed to survive the break-in, even if not much else of the store did.

"It seemed like they all came at once. I don't know why here, why they came to a liquor store, but that's what they did. It wasn't a trickle of people showing up, but like a wave, a hundred or more. A lot came through the front door, which was unlocked—I mean we're twenty-fours a day here, but that wasn't enough. I was yelling at them, and I'll probably lose my job for saying this on TV, but yelling at them just to take what they wanted and to leave. That wasn't enough either, though. They pulled the bars off the windows, smashed the glass. Two guys started a fire in the back that ate up a lot of the store, but luckily the overhead sprinklers came on. It was just all at once, everything, all of them, they just came on."

This happened two days after the letter was found, and it's not the only area in Atlanta where this type of mass looting has occurred. The mayor held a press conference this morning, saying:

"We were, unfortunately, caught off guard. The vast majority of the people who live and work in Atlanta have been law-abiding, upstanding citizens. The actions of a few are what caused this, and the police force, which begins with myself, did not foresee it happening. We were caught with our pants down, as they saying goes. It will not happen again. We are strengthening the police presence on every major intersection in Atlanta. These police aren't there to arrest those doing what they should be, they're there to stop those that have decided the law no longer applies. It does apply, and we're going to show them."

I spoke with the police chief, and the arrest rates have skyrocketed. It's not all burglary and theft. He told me rapes have increased tenfold and murders are coming in twice as fast. He declined to have an interview, but said I could quote him. "It's like every hoodlum in the world decided they couldn't be stopped because Matthew Brand hasn't been stopped."

Last night a young lady at the age of seventeen was pulled out of her car at seven-thirty pm, while stopped at a red light, and raped on the street. Cars passed and no one did a thing. The police presence the mayor spoke about had not been put in place yet. That young girl died from complications at the hospital just before the mayor's press conference took place.

The President met with world leaders yesterday, dignitaries from six nations flew in to discuss this letter and what it might mean. As of now, the President is allowing no other foreign nations to establish a police force on United States land, and in his own press briefing yesterday, he said this:

"I know people are scared. I know they see this man, and they think back to four years ago when the whole country was in a panic, and then they think back ten years before that to nearly the same thing. They're thinking, the government can't stop this guy. The government can't capture him, the government can't even kill him properly. Let me be clear. We can stop him, but we're not trying to capture Matthew Brand this time. Today, I received approval from Congress to declare war on a man who has declared himself a sovereign nation, where the laws of the United States, and indeed, the laws of the world, do not apply to him. My goal, this government's goal, is not to capture anyone, but to put to death this man who has caused so much harm and instilled so much fear.

I want to talk about that fear some, too. We're seeing on the news now about riots, about rapes, about murder, about mayhem. This isn't who we are. This isn't the America that I was brought up to believe in. It's not the America that people fought and died for over the course of two hundred years. Those people gave their life so that we could have freedom, so that we could live free from fear—from outsiders and from ourselves. The enemy that we're looking at right now isn't Matthew Brand, though. The enemy is ourselves. This fear of death, this fear of Brand, is turning us all into his puppets. It is allowing him to create the mayhem that will strain our police resources. Instead of searching for Matthew Brand, we're policing ourselves. America didn't become the strongest nation in the world because we allowed one man to dictate what we did. No, we became the strongest nation in the history of the world because we refused to allow that to happen."

The world is seeing this differently than the President, however. This is not a United States problem, say other leaders, but a world problem. Their argument is if Matthew Brand is able to succeed, it's not only the United States that will suffer, but the entire world. Their demands to be included in the search efforts, to be included in whatever information has been gathered, are heating up. *Nightline* has been told that while everyone is still polite, the politeness is being strained by the President's refusal to allow outside help into the United States.

I sat down with someone as famous in the world of physics as Ernest Hemmingway is to popular literature. I wanted to get his take on the possibilities of what Brand is threatening us with. Doctor Holland Lunz received his PhD from M.I.T. and graduated first in his class. Since then, his work has been published upwards of four hundred times in academic journals. While I don't claim to understand any of it, I am told it has pushed the boundaries of what the entire world knows about themselves and our universe.

"Can Matthew Brand do what he is saying he will do? Can he really destroy the sun?"

"You know who I wanted to be thirty years ago? Matthew Brand. I was finishing up high-school, applying to colleges, and all I ever wanted to do was make the kind of contributions he was making. So, when someone asks me can Matthew Brand do something, the first answer that comes to mind is, 'yes, of course he can'. Even with this, we had that meeting with the President, and that was my immediate reaction. I've been thinking a lot about this since, though, and I'm unsure. The issue I have, and this is an issue all scientists have, is that most of our great work is done before the age of forty. If you look at Nobel Laureates, the lot of them receive it for work done before they're forty. Really, after that magical year, your productivity, your new ideas, all of it starts to slow down. Brand is pushing sixty. Brand is pushing retirement. I don't think anyone has thought about that, but it does make me pause and wonder whether his brain can work like it used to. Without a doubt, he's still smarter than me, still smarter than anyone else on this planet, but is he smarter than God anymore? I just don't know."

* * *

Matthew muted the television.

He knew who Holland Lunz was, had read every paper the man put out before Matthew's first imprisonment. Hadn't read much of his work since though. Never met him either. Matthew had been busy changing the world when the guy was just beginning to make his bones in the realm of physics.

Even so, Matthew didn't like hearing this. The world was cowering in fear right now, the entire world. Nations were holding meetings to discuss him, to try to understand how they could stop him, and here was a leader, in a field Matthew used to dominate, basically calling him a has been. When had Matthew ever promised something he didn't deliver on? When had he ever disappointed? And yet here this man was, someone who professed to wanting to be Matthew Brand, saying that his brain wasn't good enough anymore

"Maybe it ain't."

Matthew turned to the voice, not quickly, but curiously wondering how anyone could possibly be in the room.

The old black woman from his daydream sat on the couch next to him.

"Maybe it's all gone. Not everyone is great forever." She took a drag on the cigarette, flicked her fingers and ash fell to the floor. She didn't look over at Matthew, but watched the muted television.

"What is this?" He asked, unsure if the words he spoke were only in his head.

"I'm looking for my grandson and I think you got him. Somewhere."

The man on the screen was still going through his spiel on the aftermath of Matthew's letter.

"What's your name?" Matthew asked, knowing without a doubt that this woman existed only inside his head, that he was speaking to no one.

"My momma named me Basheeba. Everybody called me Sheeb since I could walk though. Them people on the television, they talkin' 'bout you, right?"

Matthew turned back to the TV. A moment ago, his anger had been rising at the mere talk that he might not be able to deliver on his claims. Now, he was talking to someone who didn't exist.

He nodded to the question.

"They gon come after you, I suppose. Which is fine. Like I said, I'm just here for my grandson." The old woman turned her head so that her eyes met Matthew's. They were the color of clouds before a storm, a dark gray with no pupil, as if all they waited on was a bolt of lightning to crack open the rain behind them. "You know where he is?"

Matthew tapped his temple twice.

"I thought that might be the case. He wantin' out, ain't he?"

Matthew nodded, looking into those dark clouds.

"He wantin' dem women, right? Wantin' to get at 'em, the same as he did as a teenager. I knew about it. I didn't know how to stop it, but I knew about it. I tried to help the best I could but what's a ninety year-old woman to do with a fifteen year-old boy so full of cum it's practically comin' out his ears? Not a lot. That's what." Sheeb glanced at the floor and pulled a drag on her cigarette. "Well, I'mma have to get him outta you one way or 'nother, even if it means some of these women 'round here get a little more pokin' than they planned on. I ain't done talkin' with my grandson just yet."

Matthew knew what that meant. Knew what all this meant in an intellectual fashion. It meant something inside his head had just snapped. He might not be sitting on this couch; he might be on the floor, having a seizure, bleeding from his nose and a half bitten off tongue from where his teeth clamped down. He certainly wasn't sitting on this couch and having a conversation with a dead woman, a memory of thirty years ago or more. When she said she was going to get Arthur Morgant out of him, it meant that Arthur Morgant was coming to the front. It meant that Matthew was going to take a back seat to Morgant, or maybe he would have no seat at all—maybe he would be ejected from the entire ride.

"I need you to wait," Matthew said, feeling as stupid as he had ever felt in his life. "I need you to wait until I'm done here."

"You know how long I been waitin', dear? Fifteen years was the last time I talked to him, right before they put him in that freezer. But he's done thawed out and I need to talk to him, to tell him I need his report card and that only dem good grades gon keep him from endin' back up in that freezer. I can't be waitin' no longer to tell him that."

Matthew closed his eyes. He brought his hands together, folding them in his lap, and planted his feet firmly on the ground.

"I ain't goin' away foeva, dear. You know that. I might go away now but I'm gon talk to my grandson again."

Matthew focused on his breathing. In. Out. In. Out. A circular pattern that kept him alive, a circular pattern that wasn't going to be interrupted by any gray-eyed woman or any brain wiring gone wrong. His breathing, that's all that mattered.

When he opened his eyes, he was alone in his apartment, the television still silent and showing a picture of what Matthew looked like in college.

12

Twelve

"Where are you?" Larry asked.

"You don't want to know," Joe answered. He listened to his brother sigh into the phone.

"You're going to die," Larry said. "You're going to get yourself killed and it's not going to be pretty. Is that what Patti would want? This? You running around looking for that man?"

"You've seen the letter. We're all going to die if someone doesn't stop him."

"*You're. Not. A. Fucking. Cop,*" Larry almost screamed into the phone. "You're a retired landscaper with a coke addiction. You don't think they have other people on this? People that can do a better job than you?"

"How good of a job did those people do last time?"

Neither of them said anything for a while after that.

Joe was still in the bed and breakfast hotel, running lower on cocaine than he would like. He had his computer on, Google loaded, but nothing typed into the search bar. How many hours had he been sitting like this? Alternating between lines of cocaine and typing in a few words before deleting them just as quickly? Another day had passed since he visited the Holy

Ground, as he was thinking about it. Another day and, if he was honest with himself, nowhere closer to finding Brand.

"What are you going to do that they can't do, Joe? If you can tell me that, I might say, 'you know, he's right. The bastard took his son, and if he can do this better than the cops, then he has every right to be out there doing it.' So what can you do that they can't do?"

He could snort a hell of a lot more cocaine than they could, he knew that. Joe took the phone away from his ear and bent to the same white crusted plate he'd been using for the past two days and took up another line.

"And if I say nothing, and I come home, what then? Just live in your basement some more? That's if Brand doesn't accomplish what he says he will."

"Maybe. Maybe you live a few more days. Is there anything so wrong with that? Just tell me, what you're going to do that they can't do."

Maybe Larry was right. He was holed up in a hotel room, snorting blow and making failed attempts at Google searches. He'd been up for two days, and what did he have to show for it?

"I can't stop. I can't just not look for him."

"Yes, you can. You can come home and you can let the police find him."

He'd spent the last two years tracking this man—watching, waiting. Brand wasn't going away forever, Joe never believed that. Joe had seen the man face to face and understood that what drove him went deep, that there was no cure for what Brand had caught. And now Brand was back, and he had let the world know his plans, and after all these years, Joe was doing nothing more than staring at computer screens and buying bags of cocaine. If this was it, if this was all he had in him, why not go home to his brother? Maybe get clean, maybe not, but why even stay out here spending money that would run out sooner or later while making no progress?

There was a point in time when his mind had been clear. A point when it wasn't cocaine that kept him up, not entirely, and the same drive which he saw in Brand also ran in Joe. When he first started this, coming out of Larry's basement like someone leaving Plato's cave—finally understanding what life actually meant—he made more progress than the police had in the previous year. He had pictures of Arthur Morgant. He had bank account numbers. There was no doubt that Morgant was walking around, and no doubt that Brand was inside that body. Joe had even figured out Brand was most likely in the Northeast portion of the United States, which had proven out.

So what could he do next? Sniff another line and type in a few more words?

"I had him for so long and now I've lost him," Joe said.

"You don't have to be his slave. That's what you are. Your mind is his slave."

Joe stood up from the bed unconsciously. Something in that word shook his brain. Something about the word slave sparked some cocaine coated brain-cells.

Joe started pacing.

"What's a slave?" He asked.

"What?" Larry said.

"Just tell me, what is a slave?"

"You do what your master says. Someone not paid. Someone forced to do labor. I don't know, man. You're a slave because he's forced you to forsake your own life. He is your life now."

"Good. Slaves don't have choices. They do what they're told." He was walking fast now, ten paces one way, about face, and ten

108

paces back. "This thing Brand is doing, it's huge, right? I mean, you're looking at fifty-five people that have to basically give up their lives for him. Where's he going to get those people? He needs slaves."

"You sound *absolutely* insane."

"If he had slaves, you know, people willing to go ahead and die, this wouldn't be a problem for him. He could blow this whole place up without ever having to worry about being caught. Where do you get slaves from?"

"I think I saw that Wal-Mart has some on sale... Are you listening to yourself, Joe? You're rambling, man, rambling harder than Hunter S. Thompson did on his worst day."

Joe heard nothing his brother said. He paced, back and forth, back and forth, a single "IImmmmmmmm," coming from his mouth into the phone.

"You there, man?" Larry asked.

"There's only one type of slave trade anymore. Only one I can think of. Human trafficking. Sex slaves."

* * *

"You stupid, stupid, man," Matthew said. "You stupid, stupid, little man."

That goddamn Art Brayden.

"No. Your goddamn pride. Your arrogance as always," Matthew said. The crosses. Convincing Brayden that he *would* listen to Matthew. That they were going to put his message out no matter what he had to do. And now, because of that, Matthew had a new problem.

The local cop turned FBI agent was going to find him that way, or at least try to. Jake Deschaine, a nobody until Art Brayden walked into his life and promoted him about fifty levels up, had decided that he was going to look into the lumber market. He

109

was going to check and see if Matthew had bought the crosses all at one spot.

And. Of course. He had. Because he had been in a rush, because, as always—

You needed to show everyone how great you were, honey, Rally said. How long had it been since he heard her voice? The old black crone showing up first and now Rally had decided to say something. Saying, in her sarcastic way, that despite all his brains, he wasn't always ahead.

"Not right now," he said aloud, talking to Rally as if she was actually in the room with him and not something in his head. Rally was right though, he had wanted to show Brayden that he wasn't in charge, that his whole organization didn't matter at all because Matthew Brand had decided the world would die, and also that the world would know he killed it. So Matthew had gone to the most obscure place he could find, placed his order, and loaded all the logs up into his white van the very same day. Luckily, and it was looking very lucky right now, Matthew had made at least one smart decision this whole time. The minute he found out about Jake Deschaine leaving Texas, he set up a program to tap his cellphone. No one even thought to issue the man an FBI phone. Why would they? He wasn't an employee. So everything that came through Jake's phone was loaded into Matthew's computer.

"They've been scraping the lumber for DNA, hoping to maybe match up a hair follicle with DNA we already have in the system, kind of back track whoever sold the wood to him. As far as I know, though, no one's actually tried to look up where the wood was sold, because it's wood that is found in almost any hardware store. You could literally go to four hundred hardware stores in the northern part of Mass alone. You think you're going to find something here?"

"I don't think it will hurt to look. He didn't have the logs just lying around, so someone sold them to him, and it probably wasn't some criminal who would be in our system. I doubt he would go to a chain like The Home Depot because of their tracking methods. He probably looked at a Mom and Pops, somewhere that deals in cash and not a lot of back end systems to check things. It's worth a shot, because if I'm right, then the Mom and Pop would definitely remember him better than a chain would."

"Go ahead then. How many people do you need?" Brayden told him.

"Maybe five, just enough to help me call lumber stores in the state."

And, Art Brayden, with wisdom granted down from God, gave Jake the five men and they had begun calling this very day. Matthew knew Jake hadn't called the correct number yet, but he didn't know about the other five—they could already have found the shop, the man and his fat wife, and Matthew could only imagine what came next. Probably, Deschaine would find the exact day Matthew bought them, then he could check traffic cameras for the white van up and down I-85, and at some point, if they went slow and looked close enough, they would find him. Then they would look at the license plate and then they would track it to the fake name it was registered under and from there things would unravel quickly.

Had he done it a different way, had he not used the crosses as some symbolic gesture of bullshit, he wouldn't have to worry about any of this.

You can take that all the way back, can't ya, hun? If you hadn't decided to burn down that restaurant, I might still be alive today.

Rally didn't say it with malice, but with a light cheer in her voice. Teasing as she had done so often in life.

"I don't have time," he told her. He didn't have time for Rally or Sheeb today. He had time to drive two hundred miles south, find an old man and an old woman, and make sure that they never spoke to anyone ever again. That's all the time Matthew could make for the day.

* * *

Quillian Woodall looked at himself feeling just a tad bit uneasy. He'd been feeling uneasy for days, if he was to be honest. Maybe up to a week. He hadn't said anything to his wife yet, but he felt the urge to bring it up growing stronger and stronger. Even now, at five in the morning, brushing his teeth, looking in the mirror, he couldn't stop thinking about the wood he sold that man. Twenty pieces of lumber, all of them the same size.

And those crosses. Ten of them. Twenty pieces of lumber built into pairs.

He'd seen the news, and to be honest, it made him hate being seventy years old. The picture of the black man they kept flashing up looked similar to the man he sold the wood to, but he couldn't remember if it was actually the same man. Blacks, and maybe God didn't like Quillian saying this, but they all looked the same. Add to that the fact that Quillian wouldn't remember what he ate for breakfast each morning if he hadn't eaten the same thing for the past forty years, and it made for a tough time to remember exactly who he had sold those boards to. The news said to call the police if anyone had seen the man, but had Quillian seen him? More, what could they do about it now? The man, if he was the person the police were looking for, would have certainly paid cash, and this was a week ago.

Could Quillian get in trouble for not coming forth sooner?

Maybe. His Dad never liked the cops and neither did Quillian. He tolerated them well enough, but he wasn't one of those people who considered them heroes. Quillian remembered the dogs in the sixties, how the cops had used hoses on the blacks. Quillian didn't get involved with any of that, no, he was apprenticing at the lumber shop he still owned, but he remembered it—and he wasn't fond of it. The people that everyone said were heroes after 9/11 had once used fire hoses on children younger than ten. For being black.

Mary walked into the bathroom behind Quillian and grabbed a washcloth. She wet it, rubbed a bit of soap on it, and started washing her face.

"Mary, you been watching the news at all? Reading it?"

"I see what you leave on when you pass out in your chair, but I just turn it off."

Quillian spit his toothpaste into the sink and rinsed his mouth out. "There's this guy now, I forget his name but he was pretty popular a few years back as well, and he's saying he's going to do some pretty bad stuff and that the police can't catch him."

"That so?"

"That's what the news says anyway. They keep putting this picture up of him."

"Oh yeah? What's he look like?" Mary asked.

"He's black."

"That's normally the type to do it." Mary bent down and started washing the soap off her face in the other sink.

"That's not exactly a Christian thing to say, is it?"

"God respects honesty," she said, patting her face dry. She walked out of the bathroom to get their breakfast on the stove.

You did a fine job there of letting her know you sold some wood to a terrorist. Fine job, Quillian.

Did he sell to a terrorist though? That's what he wanted to find out. They'd rigged up the security cameras in the store so that it was all digital now. Quillian didn't know what the hell that meant except he didn't have to put a new tape in every two days and that he could keep the recordings a lot longer with a computer.

He hadn't used any of the security cameras in the past twelve years. There was a minor break-in twelve years prior, but it was just kids playing around. Broke the plate glass window and that cost a little bit of money. That's all though, just money, and the older Quillian got, the less he cared about it. He could, if he wanted, go in today and pull up the recordings from a week ago, could try and get a better look at whoever came in. Hell, he could call that guy up who sold him the new recording contraption and ask him to do it. That's what he'd do. He'd look into this a bit more himself before he decided to call the cops on a customer.

* * *

This thing was a headache.

Quillian firmly believed that if God had liked technology, he would have invented it. But no, the Garden of Eden had no Internet service. There weren't cellphones, and there surely weren't digital security cameras either. The Devil created technology; Quillian was sure of it.

He thought he finally had the correct picture up though. He'd been searching through the computer for the last hour, clicking this and that, trying to type in the correct date but never knowing exactly where to type it in at. He felt like this whole technology rush had just come on too quick. He couldn't adjust. Mary didn't even try. Quillian didn't think Mary could even turn this computer on, and she was completely fine with that. It was him, the fool, always trying to keep up, always trying to figure out what the world was creating.

He should let it go. It was more of a headache than it was worth. Especially for a customer. The man had paid him money for wood and now Quillian was thinking about turning him over to the cops because he bought twenty long poles and then a day later some crazy person decides to murder and string up ten women? Maybe Quillian should shut down the store and move into a nursing home, just tell Mary he had enough and couldn't cope anymore without someone looking after him day and night.

She'd just ask, "What do you think I do?" and go on with her day.

Anyway, Quillian was here with the tape pulled up and there really wasn't any sense in daydreaming longer. He pressed play on the computer and watched. The black man entered, and wow, Quillian's memory had deteriorated more than he thought possible. The man was wearing a baseball hat, so the camera couldn't get a decent angle on his face. He was black, that was sure, and tall, but was it the man the news wanted everyone to know about? How in the hell could Quillian know by looking at this?

"What are you doing?" Mary asked. "I'm running the register by myself."

"Then who's running it now if you're in here griping at me?"

Mary leaned over his chair, looking at the computer screen. "What are you looking at?"

"I just wanted to check up on a customer, that's all."

Mary looked a little closer and said, "A black customer, huh? And I'm the racist?"

Quillian shook his head, definitely not wanting to go into

it now. The whole thing had been silly. Dumb. The news, that's all it did anymore, was get people to start worrying about things that they really had no business worrying about at all. The man paid, didn't tried to rob anyone, and whatever he did with those pieces of wood after, that was his business. It was the government's business to stop criminals and Quillian's business to sell lumber.

"Come on, let's get to the front," he told Mary, standing up from his chair.

He walked from the office, Mary in tow, and stepped out into the aisled store. Not as big as a Home Depot by any means, but to hell with Home Depot, and God forgive him for swearing. People just didn't understand what the corporations were doing to America and Quillian couldn't really even describe it. He would try, of course, but he ended up just getting angry and not making a whole lot of sense, at least according to his wife. Fine. That was fine. People could shop at huge corporations if they wanted, Quillian would just keep selling his lumber in his store until the whole world said they didn't want his store anymore—

Quillian quit thinking because the tall black man was standing ten feet down the aisle in front of him. The man was turned, looking at the merchandise, nails apparently. He wore a hat and sunglasses this time. It wasn't even noon yet, who wore sunglasses before the sun was really even up?

"How are ya doing, sir?" Quillian said.

"I'm doing well. How are you?" The man asked, not turning away, but still looking at the nails. Comparing prices, maybe.

"Doing fine. Anything I can help you with?" Quillian was going through his normal routine, but nothing about this felt normal. Mary had taken another aisle and gone back up to the register, so she wasn't seeing any of it. Why was this man back here? Why on the very day that Quillian decided to try and look at the security tape had this man come back to the store?

"Well." The man put the nails back down in their container. "I was wanting to know if anyone had come around here asking about me?"

"Excuse me?" Quillian asked. The answer felt preposterously stupid but was the only answer that came to his mind. The fight or flight response had been activated but Quillian felt like he couldn't move. Like this man in front of him was a car's headlights and he a deer.

"Anyone called asking if you've sold any type of lumber to a black man lately?" The man was walking towards Quillian now, and Quillian's seventy year-old feet just wouldn't budge. He wanted them to, wanted them to run like they had when he was sixteen and had egged a house in his neighborhood, the owner coming out and trying to chase them but being too old, just like Quillian now.

The black man stood in front of him, not taking his glasses off, looking down on him. "Has anyone called looking for me?" The man asked once more.

Quillian watched as the man's hands reached up to Quillian's head, and after a sharp, quick pain, Quillian watched no more.

* * *

Matthew looked down at the woman. She had put up more of a fight than the old man, but that hadn't mattered in the end. He could still see her chest moving up and down, so he hadn't killed her quite yet, and why not? Why was he letting her live?

Oh just let me have her once. Just once. Just let me touch her once.

The words rose up in his head like hot water from a geyser, shockingly fast and making everyone around it pause and stare. Those weren't Rally's words. They weren't Sheeb's words. This was Arthur Morgant himself speaking up.

Matthew felt his cock harden. His stomach churned at the same time. He couldn't pull his eyes away from the old woman nor could he stop the dual thoughts in his brain. He saw her as an old, fat woman—wrinkled, dying, and used up. He saw her as flesh, as something to be used, to be used carnally and then to be discarded. He saw her as an entity to be used, but one that should be used with a purpose. He saw that the purpose, the only purpose all women should be used for, is for one's own pleasure.

His own thoughts colliding with Morgant's.

His dick pressed against his jeans with a force that strained the zipper.

"Don't do this. Don't do it. Think. Think. Think." He repeated the mantra to himself. DNA. Without a doubt, if he raped this woman here, now, there would be something of him left over when the cops arrived. He couldn't hide it all unless he burned the whole place down.

Then burn it down! Burn the whole fucking thing to the ground, just let me have heeerrrrrr!

It was insatiable.

It was unspeakable, what was being asked of him.

And still, Matthew pulled his pants down and climbed on top of the woman that was barely breathing.

13

Thirteen

Art placed the mask over his face as he stepped out of the car. The building still radiated off heat and smoke, despite water soaking the entire place. The store must have gotten hot, real hot, because there was nearly nothing left. Everything inside had gone up, and by the time the fire department arrived, their main job was to keep the flames from spreading to other stores. They had let this one burn out.

"How many bodies?" Art asked the first cop who came up to shake his hand.

"Two. The owners, Quillian and Mary Woodall, been residents here their whole lives."

"Jesus Christ," Art said, looking over the burnt sign that used to proclaim Woodall's Wood, but now lay on the ground before the store, a black mess. "You going to be able to find anything in there at all?"

"Doubtful. It's still too hot to send anyone in, but this thing burnt for a while."

Jake updated Art on everything during the ride down here. The fire began five hours ago; it took them three hours to get it under control, and now everyone was waiting outside as the fire department tried different techniques to cool it all down.

It was not lost on Art that he had relieved Allison Moore of her duties for something extremely similar to this. Maybe this was a bit less public, but not by much. Art turned away from the cop and started walking back to the car. Jake turned and walked in stride.

"Well, you were right about how he got the wood, just too late in finding out who he bought it from. Why the fuck didn't you ask for more people?"

"I guess I didn't think he would think of it."

Art stopped and turned to the kid. Both of them wore suits, both of their shoes had picked up ash during their short walk across the parking lot of the late Woodall's Wood. "You didn't think *he* would think of it? What the fuck do you mean, exactly?" Art had never spoken to Moore this way, and maybe that's because the whole world hadn't been on the line back then, just a few dead cops. Or maybe it was because he liked Moore, respected her. Maybe it was because Moore was older, not in her late twenties, and not picked up off the street in the greatest act of kindness seen since Jesus himself was healing people. Art didn't know, but what he did know is what the kid said made no sense at all. That Matthew Brand would not think of what this young, once upon a time detective kid had thought of?

"I thought he had moved on. I thought he was, I guess, focusing on what came next." Jake didn't look down. He and Art stared at each other, eye to eye, and that was something at least. Looking down, putting his tail between his legs, Art couldn't have stomached that.

"I need you to pay attention to me now, Jake. This man, I don't care what he says on the phone to me. I don't care what the news stations say about him. I don't care if he's losing his mind or lost a goddamn step. He. Is. Better. Than. You. You hear me? He was better than Moore, who was better than you. Everything you think of, just because I haven't thought about it, don't assume he hasn't. He will, or he has, or he is. Do you think heads of nations are calling the President daily because they're worried about some Ted Bundy style serial killer? They're calling because everyone in this world, apparently besides you, sees the big picture; that we are dealing with a criminal unlike anything ever seen. So, for the future, I'm going to need you to assume that he's already thought about whatever it is you're wanting to do. Ask for more fucking men next time."

Art walked away to the car, leaving the smoldering building behind him.

* * *

Jake wasn't crying, but he was close to it.

Where did you cry when you were constantly working? It was a question he had never asked himself. He had, at least, managed to hold off these emotions until he managed to get behind the local police station the FBI had co-opted during their brief visit. Now he stood behind the building, hands in his pocket, and looked out at the woods surrounding the back of the building. Art was already heading back to Boston and Jake would be returning soon.

He hadn't called his father yet. He wanted to, but what was he going to say? *Yeah, you left the country because I've been assigned to the Brand case, and no, I haven't been able to do a single thing to capture him yet.*

His dad wouldn't care. His dad would tell him it was okay and just to keep plugging away. That didn't *matter* though, what mattered was that he would be calling his dad without any forward movement. He would be calling his dad letting him

121

know that he was at a standstill and that whatever trust his parents had put in him was misplaced, because he wasn't able to produce.

He couldn't be mad at Art because Art was right. Jake had acted stupid, had been naive and vain in thinking that Brand wouldn't consider killing whoever sold him the wood. In fact, Jake was surprised now that Brand hadn't done it earlier. He was surprised that the married couple had lived as long as they had with Brand knowing they were possible liabilities. Jake could deal with the reprimand. It wasn't that which had him back here fighting tears that wanted to well in his eyes.

The idea had been right.

His execution wrong.

The idea, had he moved quicker, might have led him some-where. There were a lot of routes to go with once they knew which store Brand bought at and when it happened. Instead of moving closer to Brand, though, Jake's hands were in his pockets and he was feeling a light breeze against his cheek. Instead of checking video recordings of major highways on certain dates and times, he was standing with his black shoes on grass, looking at the woods before him. Instead of making progress, he was doing nothing.

He couldn't call his father with that message. He might be able to call and say something else, but not that he was standing still. Not that he had no other ideas.

Jake closed his eyes and lowered his head.

Take this moment. When you go back in that police station, you get your things, and you head back to Boston. This isn't over. This was one mistake and not one with your mind, but with how quickly you moved your hand. Your mind is there, just like Moore's was. Your mind is there just like your dad's. You go back to Boston and you get back to thinking.

* * *

Joe had gone back to Boston. He didn't know exactly what he needed, but he knew he wouldn't find it in Licent. He thought a prostitute might be the best place to start. If there were any prostitutes in Licent, they certainly wouldn't know anything about what he was looking for.

He went back to Boston and back to the same hotel he stayed in previously, spending the same three hundred dollars a night. He hadn't checked his bank account in months, and while he had been a bit frightened about looking at it before, he didn't care that much now. He didn't think he had enough time left here to actually drain the account fully. He might get close at this rate, but close wouldn't matter when he was dead. He really didn't know how many nights he would even be in this hotel room. If things went fast, he might never be in another hotel room again, or he might be in jail for the questions he planned on asking the prostitute when she arrived.

Sometimes he drew when he was really coked up, like he was now. He sat at the wooden desk in his hotel room, the single lamp on the table casting the only light in the room. A sheet piece of white paper sat before him, and a pencil in his hand. He scribbled on the paper, not drawing anything discernable, but shapes upon shapes. Circles that built off squares that connected with straight lines. All of it slowly taking up the entire paper. He didn't know what he was trying to create, didn't know if he was trying to create anything at all.

He was married for six years and had never once seen a prostitute. Hell, he'd barely watched porn if Patricia hadn't been involved. Now though, four years after her death, he was about to see his first one, but not for sex. He couldn't remember what Patricia's voice sounded like anymore. He hadn't been able to remember it for the past two years and at first he had sobbed and sobbed and then accepted it as reality. His wife was gone from this world and somehow his mind was erasing her as well. Except for the ability to continually see her death. His mind wouldn't do him that favor, apparently. Larry always asked him what Patricia would say, had been asking the same question for years, and Joe never once told him he didn't know because he couldn't hear her voice anymore. He didn't know what his wife would say about him sitting in this room, drawing an unfocused picture with an open bag of cocaine lying on the bed behind him.

What would her voice sound like?

Would she be terrified at the person he was?

Would she understand it? Condone it? Pity it?

This was all for her and yet he couldn't figure out what she would think of it. He thought he remembered considering this question when he first started out, years ago, but a lot of drugs and a lot of time had passed since then. He thought he remembered himself facing the fact that she would want him to live more than anything else, but pushing that fact away because there wasn't anything left to live for.

Was that memory true or was that Larry guilting him in some way?

Joe didn't know. He knew he was in this room, wearing out a pencil, and waiting on a prostitute to show up so that he could ask her some pretty insane questions. His wife wasn't here, she wouldn't ever be here, and even if this was all for her...

Joe didn't know how to finish the thought. It was for her. And so he would continue it.

He heard the soft knock on the door.

* * *

The woman was beautiful, Joe wasn't going to deny that. How long had it been since Joe had a woman? He would have to think back to Patti and try to remember the last time they made love. Four years and two weeks maybe? He tried not to think about shit like that, and when he did, a bit of cocaine kept the thoughts at bay. Here was a woman though, in his room, and looking like God himself may have sculpted her. And he could have her right now, the money was in an envelope on the dresser and she was already on his bed with her legs crossed.

"Party favors?" She asked, looking at the lines of cocaine laid out on the dresser next to the money.

"You're welcome to them if you want them," Joe said.

"I'm okay for now. What's your name, babe?"

Joe hadn't thought a lot of this out. It really had been a lightning bolt of thought that struck him while he was on the phone with Larry and then he simply rushed to make things happen. He found a call girl, got her up to the room, and now planned to start asking her questions about the sex trade. He hadn't planned on whether or not he would tell her his real name or anything else nearing the truth.

"Joe," he spit out, unable to come up with anything else.

"I'm Sally, Joe." The woman extended her hand. Joe accepted it, shook, and released. "You want to have some fun?"

He did. God, he did. And it would be so easy. He could roll around on top of these covers for a little while, probably no longer than five minutes if he was being honest with himself, and then pay her more money to talk.

Joe saw Patti's eyes. Deep in his head those eyes burned all the time, unable to turn off. Eyes that knew what pain felt like, eyes that said, "Oh, God. This is it. This is everything. It's all

125

over and there is nothing I can do." Eyes that said without a single word that someone was slitting their throat open and that blood was starting to poor down to the floor.

Whatever desire had built up inside Joe died.

"I'm really not looking for fun, ma'am. I'm looking for information more than anything."

Sally laughed. "Babe, I'm not an Encyclopedia Britannica. This isn't college unless you're looking for some physical education. That's the game I play, not whatever one you're trying to. So if you're not interested, let's go ahead and part ways with no hard feelings." She didn't move from the bed, didn't uncross her legs to stand, only smiled at Joe.

"That's three hundred dollars over there in the envelope. It's yours just for walking up here. That cocaine, that's yours if you want it, and if you don't, that's fine too. I don't need sex, and if you're not someone that can help me, then I'll just move down the list of girls. If you can help me find what I'm looking for, I'll give you ten grand, cash."

The woman's head tilted slightly to the right, but her smile didn't disappear. She wasn't an amateur at this from the looks of it. Joe saw she wasn't fazed by what he said, although she might not be enthralled either.

"Ten grand. Not an outrageous sum, but nothing to sneer at either. What are you looking for?" She asked. "A girl? Because I can go ahead and tell you, honey, I'm not in the business of giving up anyone's name for money. If they're working girls, they're working girls because they want to be. Pray to God that she comes home because He'll act faster than I'm going to."

"No. Not a girl. I...well, I don't even know how to say it, really." Joe didn't think, he just walked over to the dresser and put his nose to one of the lines of cocaine. When he stood up he was no longer looking at the prostitute, but at himself in the mirror. He didn't look in mirrors much anymore, and this was why. He could see the bones move at his temples when he opened and closed his jaw. His cheekbones were stark and the bags under his eyes dark. He didn't really want to see what he looked like when he took his shirt off. He'd caught glimpses, but that was all. To stare at it like this? He might have to ask himself some hard questions, like was he in danger of dying?

"I'm interested in human trafficking."

"The what?" The woman asked, stretching her words out slowly.

"I don't want to purchase anyone. Nothing like that. But, I want to know how it works, in the United States." He still didn't turn around. Joe didn't know if he'd rather face her or himself as he talked about this.

"Are you a cop?" She asked, the smile gone and her voice hard.

"No. I'm not a cop."

"What would make you think an escort would know about sex slaves? Do I look like I'm dressed as a slave? Do you think that you can stop me from walking out of here or something?"

Joe let his chin drop to his chest and closed his eyes. "No. I don't know. I need to find out more information and the only group of people that came to mind were prostitutes. I'll give you another five hundred dollars on top of that three if you just point me to someone that might know something."

Sally stood from behind him and walked to the dresser. She picked up the envelope and slid it into her purse as easily as Michael Jordan shot free throws. "You're an idiot, you know that? Even asking about something like this could get you killed."

Joe didn't open his eyes. "If I had a choice, I wouldn't be asking."

"How long are you going to be here?"

"Another day, maybe two."

"I might come back. If I do, have the five hundred ready. If I tell you something you find valuable, have half of the ten grand ready. You got that?"

Joe looked up, finding her eyes in the mirror. "Yeah, I got it," he said, his mouth hanging open slightly on the last word.

"Alright," Sally said and left the room with the three hundred dollars in her purse.

* * *

Matthew stood inside his lighthouse. The moon had risen outside and that was the only light shining. Very little of the moonlight managed to filter down through his machine, past his bodies that were growing in number. He didn't face the bodies tonight, instead Matthew faced the wall, his eyes open, but seeing nothing. He was having a fairly in depth conversation, even if he wasn't completely aware of the parameters.

You raped someone today, Rally said.

Did I? He asked.

Don't you remember?

If I could, I wouldn't want to, Matthew said. *Are you real?*

I suppose I'm as real as the other voices you're hearing, however much that means. I think I'm becoming more real as the time passes though, just as those other voices are.

What's happening? He asked.

I think you're dying, Matthew. I can't say for certain, but I think that you're simply falling apart. If I had to guess, I'd say your brain will stop working, and I mean including basic functions like your heart

128

beating. I think you may just forget to keep breathing sooner or later, and that'll be that. Rally sounded like she had when she told him they were getting a divorce. There wasn't any real emotion in her voice then, she simply let it be known that she thought he was losing his mind and that she was leaving because of it.

But I'm not done. I have to finish this.

Do you think I was done when you killed me? Think that I had marked off everything on my bucket list?

That was different, Matthew said.

How?

I loved you.

You showed it, Rally said.

What am I supposed to do now?

You could give up. If I was alive, that's what I would tell you. Just let it go. The world knows. You've proven yourself. They know who you are and they'll never forget your name. Why end it for them?

Matthew said nothing for a minute. *For you. For Hilman. That's why.*

Is this about us, Matthew? Is this even about you anymore? Whatever's growing inside of you—me, Morgant, the old woman—it's quickly becoming about all of us too. Hilman is a memory from twenty-five years ago. He'd be in his forties now if he still lived. You're fighting this war for a son that would have a son of his own right now. Why push it? Why not go somewhere and stop all this? Live out the last few days in whatever peace you can find in this body? Do you like raping women while they're unconscious?

Again, silence from Matthew. Finally, *there's no more peace here, Ral. There won't ever be any peace here again.*

Rally went silent then, leaving Matthew to the blankness of his mind. After a few minutes, he blinked a couple of times and then turned around to realize he was in the lighthouse, surrounded by bodies hanging on his machine.

14

Fourteen

The television was on but no sound came from it. Joe stared at the bag of cocaine he held, ignoring everything else in the room. He had a general idea that the time was late, but hadn't looked over at the clock next to him in a few hours. He was content staring at this white bag, looking at the tiny particles that he consumed and which, ironically, then consumed him. He'd sold his soul for this stuff, he guessed. Gave up what little family he had left to sniff it and run around chasing after a ghost.

The prostitute hadn't come back yet and he didn't know if she would. Maybe she showed up with cops in tow and maybe Joe ended up getting clean in a jail cell. If that happened, he was looking at probably a twenty-year stretch just for asking about sex slaves. The only way he would see Brand again was if the man showed up during visiting hours. Joe wasn't sure how he felt about that possibility; he was tired. The past three years weighed on him, especially after talking to Larry. He needed sleep for sure, and he thought he might find some tonight as long as he didn't put anymore of the white stuff into his face. This was about more than sleep, though. He was tired of chasing, tired of running after a man he couldn't catch. He was tired of looking for Matthew Brand, tired of the constant struggle.

This adventure didn't start when Moore died; it started years before that, when he told Larry he was moving out.

"Why?"

"I want to start using cocaine, and I doubt your wife will approve."

Larry looked at Joe like he was insane, tried to argue a bit, but Joe's bags were packed and a taxi arrived the next day.

That's when all of this began, around the time Dillan went missing and Joe woke up from the darkness and pain. The pain still existed although dulled by the dopamine released from the coke, but the darkness seemed to vanish. He had purpose again. In the beginning this had all felt different. He had energy, had motivation to search. Tracking phone numbers, hiring investigators, searching different areas of the country, looking into multiple bank accounts, crossing lines of legality. The first year was a shotgun blast of ideas, fueled not by gunpowder but the cocaine his dealer supplied. Endless nights and endless days, and eventually, he knew Brand was alive and active. That was enough. That was enough to keep Joe going.

Larry called and the two of them spoke, but they didn't see each other. He wasn't sure exactly what his brother would do if they were to meet up, but he didn't want to take any chances. His brother could, conceivably, try to get him committed, and Joe was much too busy to enter rehab. It was funny, really, lying on this hotel bed and thinking about the good ole days as those when he first started using and searching for Brand. Purpose. That's what he had back then. Patricia's eyes and his baby's smile, all on his mind, all the time. Now, when he saw his wife's eyes, they were only full of pain—and his son never smiled anymore in his head. Instead, he saw his child's massacred corpse on the metal morgue table.

All of this had been for them.

Except now, with Brand out in the open, Joe didn't know if he wanted to go on. His brain felt ragged. All the plans, all the great ideas, all the ways he had been able to track Brand before—to at least know the man was alive, they were abandoning him. Three years of constant drug usage would do that, he supposed. Is this what Sampson had felt like, turning that huge wheel, blind and bald? Wanting to give up and at the same time just once more to have his strength of old? Joe's strength had never been that of Sampson, but his refusal to tire had allowed him to succeed when the FBI simply gave up.

He dropped the bag of cocaine down next to him.

"What do I do?" He asked the room. No one answered him because no one was around.

Joe heard the knock on the door and sat up.

"Hello?"

"Sally, darling," came the answer. Joe looked over to the clock and saw it was two in the morning. He stood and went to the door, looking through the peephole and seeing only her in the hallway. Joe opened the door and took a step back.

"Hi."

"I'm here, have my cash?"

Joe walked back into the room and picked up one of two envelopes on the dresser, the thinner of the two. He handed it to her. "Five hundred in there."

Sally put her purse on the nightstand and sat on the edge of the bed. "I know someone that will talk to you. That's all I know. I don't really even know if this person will kill you, but I do know it's going to cost you more than ten grand. He wants ten to talk, and I want my ten for making the introduction."

"Who is he?" Joe asked, still standing.

"He is, I suppose, in the know. What do you understand about human trafficking? Anything at all?"

Joe absently picked up the bag of cocaine on the bed and pushed it into his pocket. "It's primarily in Asia and undeveloped countries. Poor families might sell their children into it. Many are simply kidnapped. That's about it."

The woman looked at her nails for a second. A dark red, perfectly done. "This is just my own personal curiosity, believe me, the guy meeting you will know everything he needs to know about you, but why are you interested in this? You doing some kind of documentary, because if so, you seem pretty clueless about anything that's going on in it." She looked at him. "You don't have to tell me, it's the money I really want, not your life story."

"I'm kind of out of options, I guess," Joe said. He walked over to the window and pulled back the curtains a bit. "I need to find someone and I can't think of any other way to do it."

"Darling, if you plan on meeting up with this guy to tell him that you want to find a friend of yours in his business, save your money and your breath. You won't come out of the meeting alive."

"No. I'm not looking for someone that might have been sold."

"Ahhh," the woman said, dragging out the vowel.

Joe turned his head. "What?"

"I don't know what he'll tell you when you guys meet, but I do know more about the business than I probably should. It's not just in Asia and shit countries like the media portrays it. It happens here, not daily, but probably monthly. Girls come up missing, and it's not because some serial killer got them or they quit the business. They're kidnapped, drugged, and sold just

134

like everywhere else in the world. It's not rampant, because if too many girls started showing up missing, someone would take notice. There are people that set them up too, of course. Escorts that befriend new girls, get them on the drugs, then call the men that come and pick them up. It's a nasty business."

Joe let the curtain swing back into its place and turned around to face Sally.

"When I say monthly, I mean, there might be one girl a month who doesn't show back up to work, and most of the time it's because they got some legit jobs or managed to convince a John to marry them. Sometimes though, it's the other." She stopped and looked back at her nails. Joe didn't know why she kept staring at them, maybe it was a habit. Her way of fidgeting when she was speaking about something she didn't want to talk about. She certainly looked more confident staring at her nails than if she had been wringing her hands together. "Listen to me going on and on. You want to hear this, I'm going to need another grand on top of everything else. That means you're going to twenty-one grand when it's all done."

Joe had forgotten about his exhaustion. Forgotten about the years behind him. Forgotten about his earlier question to an empty room. "Sure," he said.

"I've been all over the country doing this job. I'm leaving in another few months to head to warmer climates, because the winters in Boston are no joke, at all. So I have friends in just about every major city you can think about. We talk. Not every day, but we talk. Something's happening now, and it's a little unnerving. Girls are being taken, men too, much faster than ever before. Five missing from Los Angeles right now. Five. That's five people that had apartments, friends, a business, basically, and they're gone. No one knows where they are. No one has heard from them. One a month, that makes sense, most people don't want to make a living out of this. Five though, in one city, in one month? You can't even make a phone call to get in touch with them? That's not right. Another four in Phoenix. I don't know about all the cities, but I know that nine women aren't here that were here last month." She paused and placed her hand on her skirt, looking up at Joe. "You here trying to figure out what is happening to them?"

Joe sniffed, mucus or coke, he didn't know. "I might be. Or I might just be really misled right now."

The woman smiled. "The white stuff will do that to you. Oh well, time's short. Do you want to meet this guy or do you think it's better you turn around and go home? My six grand is coming off the top either way. The other five you owe me I'll collect if you make it out alive. If you don't, I suppose I'm sorry for getting you killed."

"Yeah, I wanna meet him," Joe said.

* * *

"Hey."

Joe heard Larry sigh over the phone. "Didn't we just talk? Unless you've changed your mind, I'm not sure what else we have to discuss. I'm trying to get ready for work."

What time was it at Larry's? Five in the morning?

"I wanted to talk to you, I guess. Just for a few minutes," Joe said.

"About what? You coming home? Giving up this nonsense?"

"No."

"Then what is there to talk about? I can't convince you how bad of an idea this is. I can't convince you that cocaine is killing you. I can't do anything except watch you destroy yourself, and to be honest, I'm not sure I'm going to do that anymore."

Joe stood in front of the mirror, naked now. His bag was packed, on the bed, with pants and a shirt laid next to it. Larry was right; the drug was killing him. Joe looked at his ribs practically poking through his skin. If there had been any rough ridges on his bones, they would certainly have punctured his flesh by now. His arms had once held at least a semblance of muscle. No longer. Now Joe was a skeleton with a thin layer of skin wrapped around him.

"I haven't even seen you in a year," Larry said. "These calls are the only way I know you're alive, and they really don't add anything to my life. They take a lot away, because every time we talk, I realize that you're gone forever. You're not coming back. You're incapable of coming back."

Joe didn't think Patti would recognize him if she saw him now. Maybe his face, but certainly not this body.

"So. What do you want?" His brother asked.

Tears were in Joe's eyes, distorting his vision, but he looked on into the mirror. "I'm going away. I'm taking a chance. I guess a pretty big one. I think I might know how to get to him, but I'm not sure. I don't think I'll be able to call anymore, so I wanted to talk to you one more time."

"Jesus Christ, Joe. Why? Why do this?"

Joe asked himself the same question last night, before the prostitute returned.

"Is it going to bring back Patricia or your boy?"

No. Nothing would bring them back.

"Because vengeance isn't enough of a reason to throw your life away. It just isn't. What about me, Joe? Do I have no say in this? Does me losing a brother matter at all to you, or is this only about you and your obsession?"

Joe sat on the bed, his frail body barely sinking into it. Larry wouldn't have a brother anymore. That was something Joe hadn't considered. He knew that he didn't have a wife or son anymore, but never thought what it might be like for Larry to no longer have any direct family. Their mother passed two years ago, and only the two of them were left—of course there were aunts, uncles, and cousins who never called. What of that? Was he willing to leave Larry alone with his wife in order for a chance at finding Brand?

"I can't stop," he said into the phone, the tears overflowing onto his cheeks. "I can't. I can't come home. I can't live with you guys. I can't be normal again, Larry. Whatever normal was inside me is gone, it's dead, and I can't bring it back." Joe sobbed into the phone, his hand coming up to his forehead. "I want to. I want to live with you guys and get my feet under me and get off this fucking drug, but I can't. It's too late. Brand. That's all that matters anymore. I don't sleep because I don't want to see Patricia. I don't want to see her dying. Do you understand that? I don't want her to die anymore, and so I use and it keeps me from seeing it."

He cried into the phone, words not coming, and his brother silent on the other end.

"I want to die, Larry. That's all I really want, to be done with all this. But I can't, I can't just kill myself because then Brand got us all. My father right down to me. No one would be left in my whole family that he didn't try to kill. So I've got to find him, or at least try, and hopefully I'll die while I'm doing it. Hopefully I don't have to use coke anymore and hopefully I don't have to be afraid to close my eyes. Hopefully I can finally sleep, and the only path that I see taking me there is this one. It might get me close to him and it might kill me, but both are fine."

138

Joe breathed heavily, his left hand wiping at his eyes. There was nothing else to say, nothing else to explain.

"I love you," Larry said after a while.

"I love you too," Joe answered and then hung up.

Joe lay on the bed for quite a while, losing track of time. He didn't think much, just stared up at the ceiling. He had called his brother an hour before he needed to leave, an hour before he needed to head to the bus stop. Be there at seven in the morning, Sally told him, and that's exactly what he planned on doing.

    * * *

"You ever hear voices talking to you?"

Brand sounded different, even from just a few days ago when Art spoke to him last. His voice wasn't shaking, per se, but it felt weak. Art was in his own hotel room, his computer open, looking at reports and email from around the country. He realized they were never going to be able to trace the calls Brand made, the guys in IT said his location acted like a virus, bouncing across the world and anytime they tried to pin it down, it threatened to invade their own system—which meant Brand could talk to Art whenever he wanted.

Art could always hang up, but he hadn't yet.

"Live or dead?" Art asked.

"Dead."

"Can't say I have. I listen for God a lot, but he doesn't really speak back, not with words anyway."

"You know, that's a question I was asked a lot over my life. Whether or not I believed in God, much more before I started the latter half of my life though. I guess everyone assumed I couldn't believe in a God if I was running around killing people."

"Do you?"

139

"Yeah," Matthew said. "My parents weren't extremely religious and I've never studied it as deeply as I have other things, but I believe there's something above all this," Brand said.

"Something bigger than you?"

"Yeah. Something bigger than me."

"You ever wonder why he doesn't stop you, then, if there's something out there?" Art asked. "You can't possibly think a God exists that *can't* stop you, right?"

"I don't think he cares to be honest. I don't think we matter to him anymore than other human life matters to me. We're something he created, or didn't create, but not something that plays into his thinking. If it was any other way, why wouldn't he have stopped me? You've tried twice, and each time I somehow come out on the other side, and from the looks of things, you're nowhere near finding me now. I'm not sure getting to the lumber seller would have worked, but it would have been a start. How's your kid taking it?"

Art's brow creased. "What do you mean?"

"Jake Deschaine, how's he taking it?"

Brand knew. He knew that Jake had been trying to find whoever sold him the crucifixes. How? "Why do you think Jake had anything to do with it?"

Brand chuckled. "I talk too much. I do. It doesn't matter how I know and it really doesn't matter how he's taking it, I suppose. These voices, they're breaking me down, Art. I can't even keep up with what I should and shouldn't be saying anymore."

Art typed the word 'slip' into his computer, reminding him to come back to it later, there wasn't any point in pushing right now. "What voices?"

"Now you want to be my shrink, huh? Wouldn't be my

140

priest before." Matthew said. Art kept quiet and so Matthew continued. "There are three of them, all kind of trying to convince me of different things. Rally, my wife. Morgant, and then some shade memory of Morgant's grandmother. I'm pretty sure that woman was with him all the time, physically as a child, and mentally as an adult. He couldn't escape her, and she's back now, talking to me and wanting him."

"This going on all the time?"

"No, not all the time. That would be truly unbearable. They come and go, but the coming is picking up and the going is slowing down. I think the freeze they put us in for all those years kind of atrophies the brain. Not immediately, but I think the brain gets so used to having to do almost no work on its own, that when it comes out of the freeze, it doesn't have the lifespan it once had. The same thing probably would have happened to my body if Moore and I hadn't been moving so quickly."

Art knew he was talking to a killer. Knew he was talking to the most dangerous man in the world, but he somehow was forgetting it momentarily. He found himself interested, wanting to know more, wanting to go deeper into Brand's thoughts. Was this how everyone had felt when they met him? Was this how the world became so enraptured with him and his ascent before he decided people needed to die? Art turned his computer screen down slightly so that he would stop scanning emails. Why not? Why not listen to him and learn more about this man? It didn't mean Art wouldn't kill him.

"How long do you think you have?"

"Off the record, of course?" Matthew said, laughing.

"Of course."

"I'm not sure. There's some evidence to show that intense meditation can create new gray matter in your brain, which is

141

another way of saying it makes your brain younger. I'm doing that for three to four hours every morning. It keeps them at bay, at least during the meditation. If I wasn't doing that, I'd say maybe a month? At the end of that, I might be Morgant, or I might just be a body that could breathe and do little else. I'm not sure. I'm hoping the meditation will give an extra month or two. Not long, is the answer," Brand said.

"You planned out for all that."

"Hell no. I planned for six months to a year, but I think I'll make this new deadline. Things are moving fast in my head, but I have them moving fast outside of it as well."

"That has to be the worst feeling for you, doesn't it? The absolute worst. You create this thing that is supposed to cement your greatness and end humanity, and then you're going to self-destruct before it can happen."

"Yeah, I'm going to end up being the Dan Marino of intelligent individuals, aren't I?" Matthew said.

Art found himself laughing, if awkwardly.

"Wouldn't be anything I could do to speed up this process, would there?" Art asked, still smiling. "Put your brain melt-down in overdrive or something?"

"Probably is," Matthew said, sounding much more sober. "I don't know exactly what though. You're right. This is all I have and I've got to finish it. That's all that really matters anymore, finishing this. Does that scare you?"

Art looked down at his bare feet against the hotel carpet. He was more scared than he had ever been in his life. Art was in the midst of a battle fog so heavy it felt like he might suffocate.

"Yeah. It does. You scare me."

Neither of them said anything for a few moments, and then, "Why?"

"Because you want to kill everyone," Art laughed, not feeling the least bit humorous. "Because you're going to try to kill everyone on this planet and I'm supposed to stop you. I have about seven billion lives resting on me. That's a lot of responsibility, Brand. That's something you've never had to deal with. All your brains and all your ideas, and you've never once had to deal with real responsibility. You're only responsible to yourself, and so I imagine you may have never known fear. It's hard to know fear when you have nothing to lose but your own life. That's all that you have in this, your own skin. I have the skin of my grandkids and their future grandkids. This Jake guy, his skin too. Chinese parents and African orphans, all of them are depending on me. Your motivation comes from within, all of it, but I have billions of voices begging me to succeed. Does that scare you?"

"No," Matthew said and ended the call.

* * *

At one in the morning, Art found himself out on the narrow streets of Boston. The wind was blowing, and despite it being summer, the heat had died away. He stood in front of his hotel, his hands shoved in his coat pockets. He stood at an intersection, no cars pulling through, but still one set of lights saying to stop and the other saying to drive. Art crossed the street, knowing the general direction he wanted to travel. Catholic churches abounded in Boston and he needed one now as bad as he had ever needed one before. He kept his eyes on the ground, forcing away any thoughts that tried to enter his mind. He didn't want to dwell on Brand and he didn't want to think about how bad he was possibly fucking this all up. He wanted the safety of God. He wanted to pray and he wanted to be surrounded by the Saints of the past.

143

He entered the cathedral, lights on low, and empty. Art didn't bother for the middle pews, but headed straight to the front, straight to the broken body of Christ hanging on his cross. He knelt, slowly, his knees popping as he did. He took his jacket off, then bowed his head and just as he began to pray, he heard the door to his right open.

"Hello?"

Art turned, looking at an old man, Hispanic, wearing pajamas, but still with a priest's collar around his neck. Perhaps he had put it on simply to open the door and see who the hell was in here.

"I'm sorry, Father. I needed to pray."

The man blinked a few times and then stepped out of the door and fully into the cathedral. The man was thin, probably nearing sixty, but he walked well enough. "That's no problem. I sometimes sleep here when the work piles up; it saves me the time of driving back and forth from home. Would you like me to leave you alone or do you need some company?"

Art turned his head to the statue of Jesus before him. His face looked so sad, like everyone in the world had forgotten him in his time of need—as they had. Art remembered Jesus saying, when two or more of you gather in my name, I am there also.

"I'd like you to stay, father, if that's okay."

"Not a problem. I was up anyway. Don't let anyone tell you differently, son, when you get older, you sleep less and think more, and neither of those things are necessarily good." The old priest crossed the room and sat down on the steps that Art knelt against. "Forgive me for not kneeling, I'm trying to save my knees every chance I get. What's bothering you this late at night?"

Art turned around, slowly, so that he sat too.

"Do you know who I am?" Art asked. If there was anyone in America that didn't know who Art was at this point, it might be this priest who slept at the church because he was too busy to go home. Everyone else had seen him on the news, heard him on the radio, or in some other way been blasted with who was charged to catch Matthew Brand. The old priest looked carefully, almost making a show of it, moving his head from side to side as he looked over Art's face.

"You're the man that's supposed to save us all, aren't you?" The priest asked, smiling.

Art didn't smile back. "Is that what the world sees me as?"

"That's what the news tells me. That's what the President tells me. Put my faith in you and everything is going to be okay. Are they right?"

Art looked between his feet. "You think I would be in here if they were right?"

"I don't know, son. I've never had that much pressure on me. I don't know if I would pray or curse God if that were to happen. You here to pray or curse Him?"

"I've never cursed Him," Art said.

"Not even once?" The priest asked. "Have you wanted to?"

"Of course, but you don't curse God, not the one that gave you life."

"So then why are you here?"

Art looked out across the empty pews. "I don't know. I just need to talk to Him I guess. I want to feel close to Him for a bit."

The priest nodded.

"Are you frightened about all of this?" Art asked.

"About dying?"

"About the world ending."

145

The priest went silent for a few moments and the only sound in the cathedral was the air conditioning running above.

"Does the pot become scared that the potter might break it?" He asked. "I'll curse God, but I won't question him. If he wills one of his creations to end us all, then there is reason behind it. God is not haphazard; He does not decide things on whims or let things enter His Holy Plan without a reason. This man, this Matthew Brand, he is here for a reason and I don't know what that is. If it's to kill us, then so be it. What will worrying about it do?"

"This rests on me though, Father. Not on God."

"I imagine Noah might have said the same thing. Nothing rests on you. Everything is in His hands. You do your best here, you try to find this man, you do what your job pays you to do, and then God will need to decide what happens with His creation."

"What do you think He will decide?"

A few minutes of silence passed. Art wasn't sure if his question would be answered, so he stood up.

"Thank you, Father."

He started to walk down the darkened aisle.

"Son, does the potter allow his pots to smash each other?"

* * *

Jake heard the laughter in Matthew's voice as he mentioned Jake's name. As he asked how Jake was handling it.

Jake had headphones over his ears and sat in front of his computer. He was listening to the recording for the third time, taking everything in, his eyes closed and leaning back in a chair. How had Brand known Jake was looking into the lumber?

The FBI could have a leak. That was doubtful though. First, few people actually knew Jake was looking into the lumber origination, and the ones that did weren't too keen on having the world destroyed.

What else? Was Brand hacking their computers? That wasn't impossible, he had managed to buy nearly anything he wanted off the internet over the past five years without anyone being able to stop him, but that would mean a lot of data for him to sift through. Jake saw a good bit of the data the FBI was running right now, Art less because he was thinking strategy rather than specifics. How would Matthew have known where to look, what emails to check, what ideas to follow?

Jake felt his phone buzzing in his pocket. He pulled it out and saw his father's name on the screen. He removed the headphones and put the phone to his ear. He still hadn't called his dad; he would blame it on time if his father asked, but Jake knew that wasn't the reason.

"Enjoying the sun?" Jake asked.

"Your mother's passed out right now," Pete answered.

"What time is it over there?"

"Eleven in the morning."

Jake laughed. "Jesus, you're kidding. Is she that drunk?"

"She's taken to calling it her afternoon nap, never mind that it's before noon I suppose."

"You enjoying it at all?"

"Yeah, it's nice. Good to get away from everything. That stuff that's on the news. That you?"

"Yeah," Jake said.

"Well, that makes a good bit of sense then. That man did a number on a lot of families the last time he was running loose, so probably a smart idea for us to get down here. How'd you get involved in it, or can you not tell me?"

Jake sat up straighter in his chair and pressed the pause button on the recording still running through the headphones. "Nah,

147

I don't see any reason why I can't. The head guy, Art Brayden, was down in Texas when this stuff started and he asked me to come aboard. I'm in Boston now, kinda acting like his right hand man, I suppose."

"That's one way to get a promotion," his father chuckled. "When do you think you'll find him?"

His father didn't ask if Jake would capture him. Just asked when.

"It's, well, it's tough. I was onto something, something pretty big, and Brand turned everything on a dime. It was like all my work was destroyed as soon as the man thought about it, and more, he somehow knew I was the one working on it. He...I mean, he couldn't have known that. No one knew, like ten people in the whole organization maybe, and yet *he* knew. Knew and then just put it all ablaze."

"You don't know how? Would someone have leaked the information?"

"I can't imagine that happening. You don't leak information to someone who is saying he's going to destroy all life on the planet."

His dad laughed. "That's probably true. I've seen some news reports, people are going pretty crazy in the states, huh?"

"Yeah, some places. It's not good, that's for sure. They're sending out the National Guard and upping the police force in a lot of the cities. How is it down there?"

"In the resort? I'm not sure anyone here has even heard of what's happening, to be honest. Peace, alcohol, and weed. That's what is in this resort."

"How much is the phone call?" Jake asked.

"I don't know. I'm just charging it to the room. Wanted to hear how things were going before your mother wakes up. I probably won't tell her too much about it; she'll be sober by then and start worrying. You'll get him, don't worry about that. Guys like this, they don't win. There's been a bunch of guys like this, throughout history, and in the end, they all die and the world goes on just fine for the most part. You'll get him."

Jake wasn't listening. He stopped paying attention to his father after—*wanted to hear how things were going before your mother wakes up.*

Wanted. To. Hear.

"Dad, I've gotta go. I'll give you a call back."

15

Fifteen

Matthew never thought he could fit that many people into the back of his van. Fifteen people were bound and gagged, lying face down behind him. With the first group, he bound them, but allowed them to sit up against the sides of the van. Their wrists had been tied to their feet, so there was no chance of movement. Fifteen people couldn't fit inside if they were all sitting up, so, Matthew tied them feet to wrists, and then lay them down on top of each other, like he was moving furniture rather than people. For the most part, they were silent, except when he hit a bump in the road or something and one of the girls might let off a noise through the tape around her head.

This group would put him at a total of twenty-two people. Mr. Bolden had delivered fifteen, and said he would deliver fifteen more in two weeks. If this kept up, Matthew would be finished pretty quickly. He had enjoyed his call yesterday with Art, enjoyed it probably more than Art could imagine. Matthew didn't have anyone anymore. Not a soul in this world besides the ghosts growing inside his head. Art, though, while not the smartest person Matthew had ever interacted with, was better than those ghosts. He acted as a sounding board, not to ideas, but to the feelings surrounding Matthew's impending death. It was something he never had to deal with before, the thought that he was going to die. Like a teenager, always thinking that the future was long and bright, not ever coming to grips with the impermanence of life. He understood impermanence now, understood that death was near. Matthew was a dead man walking and no amount of meditation would stop it.

There was room to be happy though. He needed 33 more people, and he would have them in less than a month. Then this would all be over.

"Why you keep going on and on like that? It's ridiculous."

Matthew didn't turn his head to the right; he didn't need to. He knew who was there, knew it as soon as he heard her voice. The old woman, Sheeb. How long had it been since he'd seen her? A week? It was different than Rally's voice or Morgant's, both of which stayed inside his head and only gave their opinions on what was going on—Rally's on how he should repent and Morgant on how he should rape.

This old woman though, she popped up looking as real as anyone Matthew had ever seen.

"What do you mean?" He asked aloud.

"I mean why you keep thinkin' so negatively. *This will all be over* and things like that. Don't you get tired of thinkin' like that? I know I did back when I was worryin' 'bout raisin' Arthur. It finally got to the point that I just had to understand the boy was gonna do what he wanted and I didn't have much choice in that. But you, always sittin' here thinkin' about dyin' and how you don't have much time, it just gets on my last nerve."

Matthew looked over, his eyebrows raised. "I'm sorry to not keep your thoughts in mind when I'm dealing with my own life, given that you don't exist."

151

"You're talkin' to me. I exist. I saw what you did back there with that old woman a few days ago. How'd that feel? Arthur liked it a lot, I'm sure."

Matthew looked back at the road. Such a long road. Eighteen hours of drive time one way, every two weeks. If the FBI was going to find him, it would be on these trips. He would hit a roadblock, or get pulled over because one of his tail lights went out, and they would find twenty women gagged in the back of his van and that would be it.

Matthew hadn't thought once about the old woman in the lumber store. He had thought about his brain deteriorating. He had thought about Morgant coming back, about him taking over. He considered the likelihood of Matthew not achieving his goal because of this new mental restraint. He had not thought about raping the woman at all, though. Until now.

She hadn't woken the whole time, and he had looked down on her as he pumped in and out, Morgant not letting him close his eyes. Matthew didn't want to look, felt his stomach turning and only finished Morgant's business seconds before he vomited next to the woman's head. Morgant had wanted to grab, to feel the old woman's tits as Matthew went up and down, but somehow—and thank God—Matthew managed to keep his hands on the floor. Suicide had never been an option for Matthew, but he thought if he had been made to grab the woman's breast while he raped her, he might have had to light himself on fire with the rest of the building.

"You 'on't want to talk 'bout that, do you?" Sheeb asked.

Matthew only stared forward.

"Well, you ain't got to, but it's going to keep happenin'. Arthur ain't done here. Arthur just gettin' started. You woke him up with that little piece of ass you gave him and he wants more, believe me. Arthur always wanted more, even when I told him he had to be careful. I couldn't control it back then, hell, can't control it now, but he wouldn't listen to me at all. You need to just let him come on and get it, ya know? Just let him come to the top, put yoself in the back there, and let him have his way with this world. You ain't gone blow nothin' up anyway, and ya know it. None of that even make any sense, just craziness you done dreamed up. I need to talk to Arthur though and the longer you keep puttin' him off, the longer it gone take. Let go of all this stuff you got goin' on and let my grandson have control of his body again. I can at least try to talk him outta all the awful things he wantin' to do. You ain't gone be able to talk him outta nuttin'.'"

* * *

The girl sat huddled in the corner, naked, her knees to her chest, her head buried between her knees and her arms wrapped around all of it as if trying to protect herself.

Arthur Morgant sat on the bed, naked too, looking at the girl.

That had been a lot more screaming than he planned for. That had been a lot more of everything than he planned for. It only lasted maybe forty seconds, and then the semen flowed from him, but even in that time the girl made a racket. He just hadn't expected all that to happen. Grandma had to have heard, there wasn't any way she didn't, and Arthur was really regretting having tried to do this here. He wasn't regretting what he did, not that at all, but just that he brought her back here and now his Grandma probably knew what was going on.

He heard his Grandma's feet on the stairs, knew that she was coming to his room. The only thing keeping her from being up here right now was her age. Ten years ago, she would have climbed the stairs two at a time and been up here after the first

153

scream. Back then though, she couldn't have imagined what the scream was about—now, she probably had a good idea, even if this was Arthur's first time.

The girl whimpered in the corner as his Grandma opened the door.

"Oh dear God in heaven," Sheeb said. "You done went ahead and messed everything up, hadn't ya?"

Arthur didn't look at his Grandma. He didn't really care too much what she thought about it; he just didn't want to get in trouble for it. His penis was still semi-erect and he made no attempt to cover himself. People might make a big deal outta all this, but he didn't really see the reason why. He'd done what felt natural and he couldn't help it if it didn't feel natural for anyone else.

Sheeb walked across the room, ignoring Arthur.

"What's yo name, girl?" She asked, her voice not tender, but as rough as it had ever been with her Grandson.

The girl only let out a soft cry, keeping her head buried in her knees. Sheeb walked closer, put her hands down to the girls face and lifted it up. Arthur saw then what he'd done. He hadn't really been able to pay attention to it during the act, everything felt like a blur, and now the memories were fading quickly. He hated that. It happened when he masturbated too, and that was why he took this step. He hoped that when he had a real girl here in front of him, he would be able to remember better. But just like when he used his hand, the memories made with the girl now sitting in the corner were rapidly disappearing.

Blood dripped from her nose, her upper lip swollen, and a blue patch growing on her right cheek.

"Oh, Arthur, they gone come for you now, boy. They gone come and they gone string you up. You know dat right?" Sheeb didn't turn around and look at Arthur, just kept her eyes directed on the girl in front of her.

How old was the girl? Arthur couldn't remember. They were in the same class at school and he lured her over here by saying they were going to study, but he never asked her age. He'd failed twice so he was seventeen now. Maybe she was fifteen.

"What we gone do?" Sheeb asked, bent over, forcing the girl's face to look up.

Arthur didn't say anything. He didn't have the slightest idea what came next, and didn't really care too much either. While the memory was fading, a sense of peace was taking hold, a sense of not needing to do anything, to care about anything. He could. Just. Be.

His Grandmother nodded to herself as he lay back on the bed, his erection almost completely gone, his flaccid penis lying against his leg.

"Alright, lil' girl. You gone listen to me real good. You ain't gone go tell no one, and to make sure of it, why don't you come downstairs with me for a bit?"

Arthur heard his Grandmother lead his classmate out of the room, the girl not struggling, not making noises, but following like a cow. That was good. That was much better than how he thought it might go. Maybe his Grandmother would raise a stink about it later, but not now, and good, because Arthur just wanted to get some sleep.

* * *

The door was open and Matthew saw thirty eyes looking at him.

He couldn't remember anything except the little girl being led from the bedroom, except a teenage Arthur Morgant lying back on the bed, his eyes closing, completely obtuse to what he'd just done. Matthew couldn't remember getting out of the front seat and coming to the back of the van.

Matthew looked around him. The sky was dark, the road two lanes with no cars on it, and he had pulled off to the shoulder. The only light around him came from the moon above, and it twinkled off the dark eyes in the van, all of them looking at the man who spent a million and a half dollars for them.

Come on, come on. We're so close now. Just let me have a couple. Just let us have a couple. You remember the last time, how fun it was.

Morgant, in his head, looking out at the womanly bodies, bound and lying on top of each other.

No, Matthew answered.

Yes, yes, yes, yes. The voice wasn't like anything Matthew ever experienced before, not the rationality of Rally or the at least somewhat clear mindedness of Sheeb. This was rage and hurt and madness—all of it rolled up into a longing for flesh. Longing for any flesh that Morgant saw. There were two boys in the van and

They'll work, they'll work if you don't want to touch the girls you don't have to just give me the boys just sink into them.

The words spun together almost like a soup, hard to siphon out the complete ingredients.

And Matthew felt himself wanting to step up, to climb inside, to take the women. One by one. To take the two boys and defile them as well. Maybe it wasn't Matthew, maybe it was Morgant taking over, but either way, Matthew felt the urge—felt it as strong as ever, only this time the heat from murder wasn't on him as well.

He stepped up into the back of the van and squatted down over people he'd purchased.

"Why not?" The old woman said from behind him, standing

156

outside. "Why not go ahead and have them? You ain't got no wife and you ain't got no woman you pokin' on regularly, and you gone just kill them anyway. So what sense does it make to sit out here in the middle of the road and argue with yoself 'bout it?'"

Matthew couldn't handle both of them at once, couldn't listen to both of them telling him to rip the clothes of the women in front of him and then plunge inside them. He closed his eyes. He could smell the stench of his captives, the smell of stale urine, of blood, of sweat, all of it mixing together to form what should have caused a wave of nausea for Matthew. Perhaps Morgant's personality was holding that back, was not letting Matthew feel the full disgusting nature of what lay before him.

"Why not?" The woman pestered from behind. "You just gone kill 'em all anyway."

* * *

Matthew carried the last body out of the van, draping the girl over his shoulder and walking the ten feet to the open lighthouse door. He lay her down on the floor, perhaps more gently than he might have two weeks ago. The girl's eyes followed him, alert, not deadened like some of the others he had brought in.

The sun would rise in another hour.

His body was a wreck. Even Morgant's near super human strength was fading now. Had this been Matthew's original body, none of this would be possible; he would have had to devise some other plan. As it stood, he had one more body to hang on his rings, and then today's work was done. He would head home and he would sleep as long as he could. As long as the voices would let him.

The other fourteen bodies all hung naked, wires through their eyes, and rough metal poles shoved through their hands and feet. Blood dripped down, pitter-pattering on the ground below. Soon their bodies would close up the wounds and the blood leakage would stop. The only difference between the newest bodies and the others he had hung previously was that the new comers possessed a doping agent flowing through their blood streams. The fourteen he had already hung tonight didn't feel anything. They were in a coma, more or less, unaware of their surroundings. Unaware of the holes in their body, unaware of their blindness.

He would do the same for the last woman.

What are you doing, Matthew? Rally asked.

Matthew didn't answer her. He was tired of talking to ghosts for tonight. He had sat out on that road, the back door open, for an hour, his eyes closed and concentrating on the stench growing from the men and women. Not a single car had driven by, but Matthew didn't have the ability to think about that potential disaster; he only had the capacity to keep from dropping his pants and moving legs until he found a hole he could enter. That's it. Nothing else. And he sat there for an hour, fighting an instinct that he didn't understand and could barely control, sat for an hour with his back to the world and the possibility of everything falling down with a single pair of headlights.

And in the end, he stepped out of the van, closed the door, and rode home by himself—no ghost in the front seat, nobody lecturing him to go into the back and have his way so that their grandson could be a step closer to returning.

So, with all due respect, Rally could fuck off for the moment, because she wasn't going to have anything great to add to this conversation. Matthew was going to add the sedative to the woman, then hoist her upwards and mount her to his ring. Then he would sleep. He was going to sleep knowing that he managed to not fall completely, not yet.

16

Sixteen

"It has to be. What other way could he have found out?" Jake said.

"Where's the phone? Let me see it."

"Here," Jake said, pulling it out of his pocket. He took the battery from his other pocket, laying both on the desk. "I didn't want any chance of him listening if I wasn't using it, so I removed the battery."

Art looked at the phone. How fucking dumb was he? If this had been going on, then it had been going on since the very beginning, since almost the day Moore showed up missing. If Jake was right, everything that Art knew, that Jake knew, Brand knew too. No wonder the homeless shelters weren't panning out, no wonder the police presence in nearly every major city in Massachusetts wasn't working. Nothing was working because Brand knew every step they were taking. He knew it as they were taking it, and all he had to do was make sure he wasn't in their heavy-handed way. This didn't take intricate planning on his part. This took their own stupidity and Art's inability to move as intelligently as a fucking monkey. That's all.

"You haven't had anyone look at it yet?" Art asked.

"No. My dad called this morning and said something that got me thinking, so I brought it in immediately. I mean, Brand knows exactly where my father and mother are right now, knew from the moment I told them to go down there."

Art sighed and placed his head in his hands, looking down at his wooden desk. "Jesus Christ. This means everything we've done over the past few weeks, every single bit of energy put into every single direction has been a waste. None of it was ever going to lead to anything because he already knew what steps we were taking. That's why the reports are empty every day, full of nothing but what was there the day before. He knew, he knows, and GOD FUCKING DAMN IT!" Art stood up and shoved his laptop off the desk, the cords taking pens and notepads with it, all of it falling to the floor. He stood, hands at his sides, breathing in and out of his mouth, looking at the mess.

"Take that phone and you get it looked at. Get every single piece of it looked at, every single bit of possible technology inside and out of it examined, and you find out if that motherfucker has been listening. You tell those IT motherfuckers I want to know within the hour. Whatever else they're doing, they stop it right now."

Jake didn't say anything else. He picked up the phone and battery, then walked out of Art's office.

* * *

"Hello?" Brand answered sounding confused, asleep.

"Wasn't sure this would work," Art said.

"Brayden?"

"Yeah, it's me. Every time you call a number pops up, and obviously it doesn't trace to anything. I just decided to call it back and see what would happen. Looks like it leads to you, huh?"

161

"Sure does," Brand said, sounding a bit less confused. "What do you need, Art?"

"Oh, I can't just call to talk like you do? I have to need something."

"No. You can call to talk. You're probably the closest thing to a friend I've got left, so I wouldn't want to put you out if you need an ear. What's going on?"

"Well. A lot actually. For the first time in a week, a lot is going on, and that feels pretty good. I think we might be able to actually stop this before you send us all into an icy oblivion," Art said. The anger from ten minutes ago had disappeared. His computer still sat on the ground. His secretary had tried to come in and clean up, but he shooed her away. He had made the mess and he was going to be the one to pick it up. First though, he wanted to call Brand. All the anger had been misplaced. The anger was thinking about the past, thinking about the work they had put in, and how it had all been foiled by Art's stupid fucking mistake. He overlooked the kid's cellphone. Everyone else in his organization had their own, and yet, the kid was walking around talking on a private phone. That was in the past though. That was the reason they found nothing on Brand until he decided to call or blow up a building. Art understood the future wouldn't resemble that. The future—once Jake returned and said, *yes, the phone was being tampered with*—would be completely different. The future would put Art in control of the situation.

"That's great," Matthew whispered into the phone. "How are you going to do that?"

Art couldn't tell if Matthew was asleep or not; it sounded like he was walking a fine line.

"I'm not sure that would be in my best interest. What are you up to? You sound tired. Your brain finally quit on you? Am I listening to your death rattle right now?"

Matthew laughed quietly. "No. Brain is still trucking along. Just resting. Had a busy three days. Busier three days than I may have ever had before, and I just need some sleep. You gotten any sleep lately?"

"I got five hours last night, but I doubt I'll be getting any tonight. Like I said, big things happening over here and sleeping will slow them down."

"How's Jake?" Matthew asked, sounding child-like. "I like him. You like him?"

"Yeah, Jake's good. Green, but good. Why do you like him?"

"You got an insecure kid on your hands, and most of the time, those kids outwork anyone else. He's probably working right now, isn't he?"

Art looked out his open door. Jake was gone, was always gone, only showing up when he had some more news to deliver. The rest of the people under Art sent emails and reports, but none of them were developing Jake's ideas. None of them thought about the lumber, even if they had been too late, and not a single soul in the entire FBI had thought about the phone. So yeah, the kid was working, the kid was always working—probably more than Art himself.

"Yeah, he's off trying to find you."

"Good. Good for him. I really do wish him the best of luck; he'd probably have a hellofa career if his first case hadn't been this one, because now he's just going to die like everyone else."

"I talked to a priest, Matthew."

"That's right, you're Catholic," Brand said.

"He's not too worried about what you're doing."

Again, the soft chuckle. "Well, one, he's not a physicist, and two, he's probably going to heaven. I wouldn't worry either if those things applied to me. Are you still worried, Art?"

Art wanted to say no, but he wasn't going to lie right now. He was worried, but also excited. Maybe the priest had been right. Maybe the creator doesn't allow his pots to destroy each other. Art showed up in Texas, without any authority to do so, and found this kid sitting down there working a case that he probably had no business working—except he had busted ass the previous two years and so his superiors made him detective. Divine Providence. Art had never seen it. He'd read about it, knew the story of Jonah, knew the story of Paul being blinded on the roads and then going on to spread the Good News far and wide. Divine Providence happened before and it could happen now. Maybe miracles weren't done with. Maybe God moved his hand when he was ready and maybe God had moved his hand with Jake, putting him in the right place at the right time, so that the madman on the other end of this call couldn't damn them all.

"Yeah, I'm worried, Matthew. I'm going to be worried until you're dead. Not in jail, not frozen, but completely dead. But I'm coming to realize something pretty important, something maybe the rest of the world doesn't see fully. You're not God. You never were."

* * *

Jake reported back to Art. He was right; the phone was wirelessly tapped, beamed up into satellites which garbled the data before beaming back down to Earth, and then bounced through an endless array of servers until Matthew's encrypted computer grabbed it up. Matthew Brand had access to everything Jake had said over the past few weeks.

There wasn't any way to trace it.

"No fucking surprise there," Art said.

The techies were fairly certain Brand couldn't listen unless the phone was being utilized, as in Jake was on a call.

"There's that at least," Art said.

The phone sat by itself in the passenger's seat of Jake's car right now, battery in. He'd spoken with Art for two hours about it, brought in other people, all experts that Jake didn't know in fields that he had never considered. They talked and talked and talked about what could be done.

"It's a God damn miracle," Art said at one point, looking at the phone on the table.

Art attributed a lot of today to God, and probably a lot of other people at the table did as well. Jake didn't know whether that was true or not. Jake did know that they had an opportunity here and all the ideas that were passed around didn't seem to fully grasp what they could do. Or maybe everyone grasped it, but they didn't know how to fully capitalize on it. Jake didn't either.

Not yet at least.

Jake grabbed his new phone from his pocket, the one now issued from the FBI, and dialed up his father, wanting to talk to him, wanting to hear something besides this case for a few minutes.

"Tell me a story," he said, so his father did.

* * *

Oh, Jesus. I've been drinking and thinking. Your mother is out with some other couple somewhere, and I'm just sitting here on our balcony with a scotch. I've been thinking about this for a while and I didn't know how to tell you, exactly. I suppose drunk isn't the best way, but I might not have the courage later. I don't know, just listen.

165

Vietnam wasn't easy. I don't really know any other way to put it. It wasn't easy. I'm not going to sit here and go into detail about what went on over there because I think too many people have done that already. A lot of people that didn't need to die, did, and that's about all there is to say on it. When I came back though, to the states, my mind wasn't right. I'm alright now, and that's in large part to your mother. Woman can get as drunk as she wants on vacation, because if it wasn't for her, I probably wouldn't be much of anything right now. Not that I'm much of anything as it is, but I have enough money in my bank account to see me out of this world and I got it legally for the most part, so that should count for something.

When I came back from Vietnam, a life like I currently have wasn't a possibility. I planned on drinking a lot, shooting some H, and having sex with as many women as I could find. That, at twenty-three, was what I considered the good life. I met your mom at a Waffle House. She was waitressing, and I was coming in and out of there every week or so. I made sure I sat in her section. Half the time I was drunk and the other half I was in there with some rowdy Army buddies after midnight. But I always sat in her section. She didn't want anything to do with me, not a thing. She served me, but that's because she had to. She wasn't necessarily pleasant about it, either. I didn't mind. She was a knockout, and trust me on this, you do what it takes to have a knockout serve you food even if you have to pay her. If you understand that, you're ninety percent ahead of every other man in this world.

So months came and went and I stayed pretty much drunk. Your mom pretty much sober.

One day I said something like, "Why don't you just go out with me? Just once?"

She put my coke down and walked off. She didn't come back the rest of the night and I didn't say nothing else about it either. When she served me the next time, neither of us mentioned it. This is about three months to me being back and showing up at that Waffle House.

So, I was drunk another night and said, "You ain't gotta be a bitch about it, but why not just go out with me? You give me an answer as to why you won't and I'll leave ya alone about it."

Now you repeat this, Jake, and you and I are going to have a lot of problems in the future. I don't know if we got a super long future to begin with given this Brand guy, but whatever future that is, you don't say a word about this to your mother. I need you to understand that, this is between us, and I don't think it'll change anything between us because everything is still the same as it was five minutes ago.

Your mom said, "Because I'm pregnant, asshole. You feel like raising some other man's son?"

And I looked at the Coke she had placed down on the table, then glanced at her belly, not seeing much of a poke—but she was only three months pregnant—and then back to my Coke. I was eating alone, thank God, because I don't know what would have happened if my Army pals were there. She went away, leaving me with my Coke, and neither of us said another word to each other the rest of the night. I got in my car, drank some of the bottle I had under my seat, and then drove home just about as drunk as I'd ever been. I couldn't sleep though, which wasn't normal, because when I drink the lights simply go out. I laid in bed all night thinking about what she said. Did I want to raise another man's son? Hell no, I didn't. I seen this video once of what happens when a male lion takes over a pride. He murders all the cubs already there, and while I didn't want to go around murdering children, I certainly didn't want to be raising someone else's offspring. She knew it too. She knew that almost everyone she met from here on out wasn't going to want to raise some other man's child, so here she was, having the child anyway, and understanding what that meant.

The whole time I thought she didn't want to date me because I was a drunk Vietnam vet. The whole time I'm sitting here thinking that everything that's going on between us rests on me and how fucked up I normally was when I saw her. Except it didn't have nothing to do with that at all, not really. Your mom had demons that I couldn't even begin to understand. She was living by herself, pregnant, and serving hash-browns on the graveyard shift at a diner.

I woke up with a bad hangover the next day. I mean I closed the blinds and didn't get out of bed for hours and hours. Just lay there, head on top of one pillow. I kept thinking about those words over and over. *You feel like raising some other man's son?* Last night the answer was hell no, and maybe it had a bit of anger in it too. Anger that such a pretty woman was pregnant with another man's kid. Anger that I didn't have a chance with her, maybe anger that I had said something so offensive, without even considering what she was going through. That morning though, with a headache trying to split me in two, I didn't feel anger. I didn't feel *Hell no* either.

I felt, *might as well give it a shot.* I mean it, son, you get a good-looking woman that will serve you food, you try to hang on.

So I waited a day and a night. The next night at one in the morning, I walked in sober. I wore my uniform from the Army, because I didn't have a suit, and I didn't want to show up looking like the asshole I was. I didn't sit down, I just stood at the counter and waited for her to walk over.

"Getting it to-go tonight?" She asked.

So I said, "I don't know if I want to raise another man's son, to be honest. Maybe I will and maybe I won't, but that doesn't scare me away from wanting to get dinner with you and seeing where it goes from there. That's as honest as I can be, and if that's okay with you, I'd like to take you out the next night you have off."

The cook turned around at this point and was looking at me too. Your mom didn't say anything right away, but she placed the pad and pen down and just looked at me. I stood there and looked back. I was incapable of feeling stupid from being stared at because drill sergeants did that shit all the time. So I stared and she stared and the cook stared too and finally she said, "Okay. I'm off tomorrow. I'll meet you here and we can decide what we want to do."

So this is probably a shit way to tell you, but if we're going to die in the next month or so, I figured you ought to know how good of a woman your mother is. She turned me from a boozing, drug using, tail-chasing little shit, into someone that wanted to raise progeny not from myself. That's you, Jake. Now, you're *my* son; you're not anyone else's son, so I don't want you to start thinking any nonsense like that. I love you and I never wanted another child, or else we would have had one.

Hell, I don't know why I told you all of this. Probably the drink. I'm sorry it's coming out like this.

* * *

"It's okay..." Jake whispered.

His imagination was blooming, a flower uncurling its petals and announcing its beauty to the world.

"You okay? Jesus, I shouldn't have said anything."

169

"I'm okay, Dad. Hey, I have to go. You may have just saved everything."

Jake hung the phone up without waiting on a response. He stared out the windshield, but saw nothing. His father—what would his father do for him? Anything. Jake knew it as sure as he knew his own name, and yet, his father had just told Jake that there was no biology connecting them. The love that each possessed for the other was based on actions alone, on belief, but not on any DNA shared. What had Brand done for his own son? He had killed for him, and now he was trying to destroy the world for him.

Jake didn't know if it was possible, if they could pull this off, but his father had just given him an idea that might put them all face to face with Brand—that might, actually, bring Brand right to them.

17

Seventeen

Joe's suitcase sat in front of him, the handle pushed down, as he waited for a Greyhound bus. He'd taken a taxi to the station, bought a ticket heading to Los Angeles, and then sat on one of the benches while he waited for the bus to arrive. He didn't know if he would make it to Los Angeles, didn't know if he was being lied to about this whole thing, only that Sally told him to buy the ticket, and after he did, someone would be in touch.

"Go to the back of the bus, sit in the last seat on the left, next to the window. If someone is already sitting there, you need to find a way to make them move. It won't be good for anyone involved if you're not the person in that seat."

Joe arrived two hours early so that there wouldn't be any problem getting whatever seat he wanted. Back seat, front seat, hell, he could ride in the baggage compartment as early as he was.

People began showing up slowly, wandering in. This was a long trip, days, and it didn't look like that many people were going to show up for it. It was cheaper than a plane ride but a lot more aggravation. Sally didn't say anything about anyone sitting next to him, so he supposed if someone sat down, that would be fine—but maybe, from the look of things, he'd have the row to himself.

What are you going to do if you get out to LA and all you have to show for it is less money in your bank account?

That possibility seemed more and more realistic the longer he was separated from Sally. Prostitute or not, the woman was a professional at getting people to believe her. When Joe listened to her, he found himself believing everything she said, that she would introduce him to someone who could give him the information he needed. All *he* needed to do was pony up the money to both her and the guy. Now though, with only ten people sitting at this bus stop, he didn't feel so confident. He wasn't going to turn around, of course, but he was beginning to think nothing would happen outside of a long trip across the country—wasting what little time he had left to find Brand.

Had he told Larry this new plan, Larry would have laughed and spelled out all the possible problems in glorious detail. He hadn't though; he only told Larry that he would be leaving, and now here he was with the sun just beginning its slow ascent to the top of the sky, without a number to call or a person to discuss any of this with.

Joe watched the bus pull up. He stood, grabbed his single bag, and moved to start the line for entrance. At the very least, he'd do what Sally said and hope for the best. What else was there?

* * *

Joe found the seat he was instructed to sit in. He did so, leaning his head against the window, but still keeping an eye on the rest of the people climbing aboard. They took their seats, most looking at something on their phones. The whole world only looked down now, none of them paying any attention to what went on around them. Joe might have been like that a few years ago, but no more. The cocaine probably had something to do with that, because it was tough to keep focused on a cellphone when you had that much powder making your brain jump. He held a pretty big sack of it in his pocket, and planned on using the restroom whenever he needed to keep the high going.

The engines started rumbling and everyone was in their seats. No one looked back at Joe. No one stood to come sit next to him. No one did a single thing as the bus pulled away from the sidewalk and the driver began making announcements. Joe was alone and leaving Matthew Brand. He was heading across the country based on some prostitute's word.

He felt sick and he felt tired, and rather than his usual modus operandi when he felt tired, he closed his eyes and let sleep take over.

* * *

Joe felt the presence next to him and woke up slowly, his eyes just barely opening. Someone had taken a seat, and from the feel of things, the man was large.

The feel of things was right.

The man must have been pushing three hundred pounds. His large, beefy arms spilled over both hand rests, pushing into Joe's area. The man seemed not to notice that he had just taken over someone else's spot, but was instead trying to rearrange his abnormally large gut into a comfortable sitting position. This involved moving his ass side to side and front to back. His head was bald and his skin the color of porcelain. His shirt was triple-x if not quadruple, with only the word ADIDAS across it.

Joe sat up a bit, trying to make room for the man who was going to take the room whether Joe acquiesced or not. He wasn't fully awake, but was coming to it.

173

The fat man looked over.

"How are ya?" He asked.

"I'm good. Tired. You mind if I take the aisle seat on the other side of you? Probably going to need to use the bathroom in a few." If Joe was going to be awake, then he was going to be high, and moving back and forth across this beast would not be easy.

The fat man cocked his head to the side. "You should get some more sleep if you're tired."

Joe saw the man's hand sitting on the arm rest, a big, flabby—if strong—looking thing. Joe watched in stunned terror as the man's hand moved with the grace of a ballerina, pulling a syringe from his pocket, and then digging said syringe into Joe's leg. He felt the piercing metal dig into his flesh and tried to let out a sharp cry, but the fat man's other hand had wrapped around his mouth, and then Joe started swimming in a giant pool of darkness.

18

Eighteen

The New York Times
Online Edition

Blackout Rolls Across North East
Explanation Not Forthcoming

At 8 AM EST yesterday morning, the power in the furthest point of Maine, a town named Cambellton, went out. No eggs for breakfast, no hot water, no lights. Cambellton, by any definition, is a very remote location. However, by noon all of Maine was affected and the outages weren't being contained, they were spreading further south. By midnight yesterday, the blackout stretched from the top of Maine to the southern edge of New York. It followed extremely strict state lines, never venturing into a state that it didn't fully black out, leading people to believe this was man-made rather than an error or accident.

It's been twenty-seven hours since the rolling blackout began and there doesn't appear to be any respite.

The Director of New York City Power spoke at a press conference today, in the state of Pennsylvania, where power still exists.

"We are unsure what lies behind these outages. Our engineers, our information technology people, everyone, is working around the clock to try and fix this problem. The President has declared a state of emergency, and we are working with every single power company from New York upwards to try and get to the bottom of this. No one is sleeping until this problem is solved."

Five hours later, the problem has not been solved and, in fact, more problems are arising. The outages sparked, almost immediately, large scale traffic jams when traffic lights shut off. This led, eventually, to hundreds—perhaps even thousands—of abandoned cars, ensuring the gridlock. Businesses have shut down throughout the Eastern Seaboard, which has led to widespread looting. Criminals are breaking into businesses, large and small, and taking everything that can be lugged out. Many large items are left, however, as there simply exists no way to transport it from one area to the next given the condition of the roads. In New York City, the police were released on foot to crack down on the crime epidemic. From dying cellphones we have captured instances of police brutality, perhaps not seen in such high numbers before. Indeed, one police officer screamed into a group of people standing outside a closed shop yesterday: "If you're outside, your head is getting busted."

The President is supposed to speak tonight, and speculations have risen from people domestic and abroad that this is linked to Matthew Brand. The manhunt is still wildly active, spreading up and down the eastern side of the United States. This newest issue has reignited sparks of outrage from foreign leaders, including Canada's Prime Minister.

"It makes absolutely no sense that the President is refusing to accept our help. Two weeks have passed and all we hear, day in and day out, is that they are close to finding Matthew Brand. We see the Director of Operations, Art Brayden, on television everyday saying that they are working diligently, but that's it. There is no other information forthcoming from Washington, and the President hasn't taken a single call from me in the past two days. Now these blackouts are literally one mile from Canada. A mile further down the road and the inaction of the United States begins to affect my constituents. I demand that the President begin to release more information and to accept help from the outside."

President Herald is supposed to comment on both the ire spreading outside of the country as well as the possibility that these blackouts stem from Matthew Brand's operation. As of yet, Brand has released no other news regarding his plans, although a suspicious fire in Massachusetts did draw the attention of the FBI a week ago.

The President will begin speaking at 7 PM EST.

* * *

"How are you charging your phone, Art? Can you tell me that, at least, since there doesn't seem to be a single other thing you can tell me?"

Art listened to his boss, Gyle, nearly snarl into the phone. It wasn't a bad question, really, because not a single outlet in Massachusetts was working, neither were any of the landline phones.

"I had someone drive across the state border and purchase a hundred new cellphones. I just keep changing the SIM card. Don't worry, I expensed it," Art said.

"I'm glad you're finding it funny. President Herald isn't. I imagine you're going to have a call from him once this press conference is over. Is this Brand or not?" Gyle asked.

That was the question the whole country wanted an answer to and Art didn't have it. No one in his entire organization could trace the source of the outage. It began in the furthest tip of Maine and then spread south, like a virus, logically infecting every touching town as it went. It didn't skip anything, it didn't spread out of control in one spot while leaving another untouched. It moved timely, orderly, downward, taking with it all electricity. It followed a system, a system that was plain and obvious, but one they didn't know the root cause of.

"I don't know," Art said, the humor gone from his voice. "I'm not hiding anything from the reports you're getting, Gyle. They're coming in hourly from engineers that are looking at the individual wires as well as people looking at this from a holistic perspective. There isn't any clue as to why the power is gone, where it's gone to, or if it's coming back. The power plants are still working, in fact, all the lights are on in every power plant in every state we're talking about, it's just that power is being directed somewhere else."

"And you can't trace it?"

"We're trying to, except, it isn't pooling anywhere. It appears to be siphoned off by the surrounding states, like the houses in New Jersey should be using the power from New York, but when we've measured it, that's not what's happening, it's just what appears to be happening," Art answered.

"So where is the power going then?"

"At some point before it is used by the surrounding areas, it's stolen. It disappears and that's where most of the engineers are looking now, trying to trace all that power. It's a huge amount, Gyle. All the power from five states just disappearing, but yet we can't find a trail."

Gyle sighed into the phone. "The President wants to know if this is Brand or not. He wants to know what to say when he gets on the television tonight and I can't go back to him with this answer. I can't tell him 'I don't know'. That's not what you tell a sitting President if you want to keep your job. I need you to have something more to me by the end of the hour. Have something of substance, Art. I don't care what it takes."

* * *

The phone lay on the table and Art stared at it. The door to his office was closed and no one should be knocking on it unless they had information directly pertaining to the power outage. This newest development was splitting his manpower. He was having to investigate the power problem while also conducting a manhunt for Brand. And, on top of it, Brand had been silent. Completely silent. Art called three times over the past twenty-four hours, and each time he heard a prerecorded message saying the customer had not set up a voice mailbox yet. Art didn't know if these engineers working below him were complete idiots or if this was some kind of miracle of nature, but he was heading to a power plant today to try and figure that out. He might even stand right over the pack of engineers, watching each movement, both to let them know how serious he took this, as well as to understand. He wouldn't get the math, wouldn't get all the details, but he had a feeling he was going to speak with Gyle again today and have the exact same answer: *I don't know.* If that's what he had to tell Gyle, he needed more information than the power was disappearing, probably on the back of a Unicorn.

It had to be Brand though.

Why else wasn't he answering? Why else had he gone dark?

And that led to the question which Gyle hadn't asked, that the media wasn't asking either. If it was Brand, did it mean they were too late? Did it mean that things had already begun?

Art wanted to pray, to head out of this Boston based building and to the church down the road, but he didn't have time. Art didn't have time for God right now. What he needed, more than anything else, was Brand. Jesus Christ, Art hadn't even decided what they were going to do with the knowledge of Jake's cell phone. No, that had been pushed to the side because millions of people were sitting in the dark. Art's resources were strained to a point of nearly breaking and Brand could give him the answer he needed with a simple response: yes or no. He was behind it or he wasn't, and Art thought that Brand would answer the question if they could just talk. The man's pride wouldn't allow him to lie, wouldn't allow him not to receive credit if credit was due.

Call him one more time, then fly to the New York power-plant. One more time.

He picked up his phone and looked up the past number, clicking on it.

It rang for thirty seconds, and then right back to the recorded message.

"God damn it," Art said, dropping the phone onto the table where it landed with a loud clack.

He stood up and walked to the office door.

"I need a flight to New York's largest power-plant within the hour," he said to one of his secretaries. He had three of them, didn't know any of their names—his regular one, the one he had used for the past three years, had gone out on maternity leave three weeks before all this started. God bless. So he had three now because they were doing almost everything for him at this point, any administrative duty from payroll to lunch.

"Yes, sir," a brunette said.

"What's your name?" Art asked.

"Kerry."

"Thanks." Art closed the door. Kerry. At least he knew one of them.

He was walking to the computer at his desk when the phone started ringing.

Please, God.

He went to it, picked it up, and knew before answering that it was Brand. *Unknown caller*, although if Art hit redial, he'd end up dialing a number that led him back to Brand.

"You rang, Art?" Brand said.

"Yeah. Was wanting to see if you'd like to catch a Red Sox game this weekend?"

"Unfortunately, I'm a bit busy at the moment," Brand said.

"You motherfucker. Is this you? Just tell me if it's you."

"Oh my gosh, such hostility, Art. I remember you calling me the other day, but I don't remember what we spoke about. I was kind of a mess, really needed some sleep, and everything you said went in one ear and out the other. Would you mind catching me up on what we spoke about?"

"As soon as you tell me if this is you," Art said, his fingers gripping the phone so tight that he could hear the plastic bending.

"Of course it's me. You didn't think I would be able to do everything I said without a large source of power. One cannot simply split every atom in fifty-five bodies with an ax, one needs a lot of energy to do it. I can't buy that type of energy in a double-A battery, so I'm having to borrow it from some of the places around me."

Art's balls pulled upwards, his scrotum shrinking, and sweat popping out onto his forehead. "It's starting?"

"Well, yes and no. Call this a dry run. I needed to make sure that my theory would work, and it is. The lights won't be going back on, because I do need to make sure my machine is going to run when the time comes, so I need to go ahead and start checking through all of it, but no, I'm not splitting atoms yet, if that's what you're asking."

Art's fingers relaxed a bit on the phone. "People are dying. You know that, right? You've plunged millions of people into darkness and they're losing their minds."

"Art," Matthew said, his voice no longer holding levity, "it's going to get a lot worse than this. Those people you're talking about, they have power during the day. They have sunlight that keeps the water clean and the crops growing. They might be scared, but this isn't anything that humanity hasn't dealt with on a wide scale basis before. What's coming, what I'm building towards, that's what should frighten them. A world with no light, only eternal darkness. If they're dying now because they're killing each other, why should I concern myself with that? This isn't an issue. This is like the eighteen-hundreds, but you didn't see massive looting, murder, or rape every night because they didn't have electricity flowing into houses. The lights aren't coming back on, no matter what your engineers do. The President is speaking tonight, and if he says you guys can fix this, he's a fool and a liar. Everything from New York up is mine now. In my world, I don't govern, I don't try to control. The people can do as they see fit."

At least Art had his answer. There wasn't any more wondering and there wasn't any more need to use up his available capacity. They could put this off to some other organization and he could

182

focus on finding Brand again.

"You know he's going to say we'll turn the lights on," Art said, unsure why he was continuing the conversation now that he had what he wanted.

"Of course. You won't though. Was there anything else you needed, Art? I'm a bit busy making some preparations."

"That's it."

"Bye, then. Talk soon."

* * *

"It's him," Art said.

"How do you know?" Gyle asked.

Art and Jake sat at Art's desk, the plane ride to New York canceled. A speaker sat in the middle of the table, from which they both listened to Gyle.

"I called him. You can run the tape if you want, it's uploaded. He says it's not D-Day, but that he's basically working out any possible kinks before D-Day arrives. He also says that the power is staying off, that no matter what we do, we won't be able to redirect back to its original path."

"For how long?" Gyle asked.

Art looked at Jake. "Forever is my guess. Until either we kill him or he shuts the sun off."

Gyle laughed. "This is getting worse by the moment. Every time I pick up the phone and talk to someone, I get just a bit closer to putting a bullet through my eye. Now I have to tell the President we know it's Brand and that the lights are going to stay off. I have to deal with hundreds of people dying nightly because, apparently, when we can't watch television we turn into animals *and* I have to talk to you knowing each and every time that we are not any closer to finding Brand. This is a nightmare."

The room fell silent for a few seconds.

"That's not entirely true, sir," Jake said.

Art looked back up, his eyebrows rising. Which part wasn't true? Jake had shown up for the meeting because Art sent him a text, but that was all they had said to each other in the past day. In fact, Jake could have been vacationing in the tropics for all Art knew—he had seen no reports, received no phone calls, nothing.

"You speaking to me or Art?" Gyle asked from the speaker.

"You, sir. We may be a bit closer to finding Brand. I think I might have something to pull him out into the open, if we do it perfectly. If he believes us, and we don't screw up on our end, I don't think he'll have much of a choice in the matter."

19

Ninetcen

The sharp smell of sulfur opened Joe's eyes.

Things were blurry, as if he was looking through goggles filled with water. He blinked, trying to bring the world into some sort of focus. Nothing on him hurt, but his entire body felt tired, weak, like breaking a pencil would be a monumental feat.

His eyes finally cleared and a lone man stood in front of him. There was a chair next to the man, a flimsy plastic thing.

"Mnuhh," Joe said, not understanding that speech was beyond him until the word exited his mouth.

"No need to talk just yet. Just sit there and relax for a few, buddy."

The man in front of him had been the man that sat down next to him on the bus.

What bus?

The Greyhound.

The Greyhound he had got on headed to Los Angeles. Then this fat man had sat down and stabbed him in the leg. Joe slowly gazed down at his leg, saw a little circle of blood just above his knee, but felt no pain from it.

Did he stab me?

Maybe. Maybe not. Where was he now? He tried, for the first time, to stand up, and realized his arms and legs had both been tied to the same type of flimsy chair that the fat man stood next to. Zip-ties on his wrists, forearms, ankles, and calves. Joe wasn't standing up from here. He was, though, remembering what happened. Sally told him to take the bus, the bus to Los Angeles, and that someone would meet him with the information he wanted. Was that this fat man? Was that where he was?

He looked around the room, his head moving slowly, like the first time he ever tried pot. He was in an old bedroom; something out of the seventies, with wood paneled walls and green carpet. The smell of the place said that a lot of life had happened in between these walls and not a lot of airflow after. There wasn't a bed though. Wasn't a dresser either, only a closed window to Joe's left.

"My name is Charles. Not Charlie, but Charles. Yours is Joe, right? Joe Welch, born Joseph R. Welch?"

Joe nodded, his eyes coming back to focus on Charles.

"You have had an interesting history, Joe. To be honest, much more interesting than probably anyone I've met. Dad was murdered by Brand. Wife and kid too. Now you have a habit," the fat man pulled out the bag of coke that had been in Joe's pocket, "and an obsession with Matthew Brand. I've been wondering myself what obsession is stronger, the one for this stuff in the bag or the one for Brand. Given that I'm someone who knows a bit about addiction, I'd guess that they're running neck and neck. Two large horses and each of them running at top speeds. What do you think?"

Joe's head lolled to the side a bit. This man had to know Joe could barely hold his head up, let alone answer. He was able to listen, though.

"What I don't understand, where I'm coming up at a loss here, is why someone who is running around looking for the most wanted man in the world would suddenly become interested in sex-slaves. It's not your fetish. So why?"

"Yahnn," Joe let out, his tongue feeling like a large furry balloon, unable to function correctly at all.

"Don't worry about it. We're going to have time to talk. Go on to sleep, I'll be back later." The fat man turned and walked from the room, closing the door behind him. Joe kept trying to look around, kept trying to stand up, but his attempts became weaker and weaker until he took Charles' advice.

* * *

Joe's eyes were open and he stared out what little of the window he could see. Moonlight shone into the corner and he saw a cloudy sky, but nothing else. The overhead light in the room was turned off and the door still closed. He heard people moving around downstairs, but was unable to shout at them. At some point during his slumber, someone shoved a gag in his mouth and a piece of tape over it. All he could do now was look out the window and breathe through his nose.

After a while he heard footsteps coming down the hall, large creaks moaning as the person moved.

The door opened and the light above flashed on.

Joe closed his eyes immediately, only to try and open them right after, slightly, enough to see who was in the room with him.

The fat man. Charles.

He walked across the room, put one hand on Joe's forehead and the other at the edge of the tape, and ripped—igniting a flame across Joe's lips. He reached into Joe's mouth and pulled out the tiny cloth that had been shoved inside. Charles turned around, folded the cloth and placed it next to the empty chair. Then he pulled the gun out of his waistband and turned back around to look at Joe.

"I want you to understand something from the get. You're in constant danger of death here. Your life means slightly more to me than a cockroach might mean to you, and that's only because your first instinct is to kill the cockroach. I don't want to kill you, necessarily. At least not yet, but the second you give me even the slightest inkling that I want to, a bullet from this gun is going in your head. You got that?"

Joe nodded, completely understanding what the man meant while having no idea what he needed to do to make sure that didn't happen.

Except stay quiet. It would be hard to make someone want to kill you if you didn't open your mouth.

"I took the five grand out of your wallet. That's half of what you owe me. We'll be getting the other half real soon or you're going to make me want to kill you, okay?"

Joe nodded.

"Now, I'm going to ask some questions and you're going to get one chance to answer me. I'm no mind reader, so I'm not going to have proof if you lied to me. All I can say is that I better not think you're lying to me, or again, it's going to make me want to kill you. Still with me?"

Joe nodded.

"Good. Now tell me, why did your put your neck out like this to learn about human trafficking? Sex slavery is what I think you called it."

Joe squeezed his eyes together tight. The answer was sprawling. The answer started with a black kid being shot down in a trashy neighborhood twenty-five years ago and ended with the bag of cocaine that Charles had hid somewhere. An infinite amount of choices during that time, all of them leading Joe to this old house, in this stale smelling room, talking to this morbidly obese man.

"Matthew Brand," came from Joe's mouth.

Charles nodded. "Had you said anything else, and I pretty much mean anything, I was going to have a lot of cleaning up to do. Blood begins to smell after a few days and I like a clean house. Next question. Why do you think the sex-trade has anything to do with Matthew Brand?"

Joe sighed. Did he tell him that it was probably a cocaine induced hallucination in which he thought the easiest way for Brand to attain the people he needed was through an underground movement that not even the government really tried to track? Did he say that he wasn't sure of anything, and that his mind had been slowly going to hell over the past six months, and this was a last ditch effort? A last hoorah to try and find Brand?

There was some logic behind the idea though—however small—and he might as well start with that. "He needs a lot of bodies. I..." Joe trailed off. "I don't know. Maybe he got them this way. He's not grabbing them off the street. He's not hunting down people associated with his son's death, because there aren't enough of them left anymore. It just connected that this might be the way and now here I am."

"I don't want to kill you yet, and that's a good thing, Joe. What do you want with Brand? What are you going to do if you find him?"

"I'll kill him," Joe said.

"How?"

"However I can."

"No one else has been able to. Why are you going to be any different?"

"I don't know. Maybe he'll kill me. I don't really have a choice anymore though, except to try and find him, to try and kill him. That's all I have left."

Charles sat down in the chair, leaning his massive arms forward until his elbows reached his knees. "You don't have much then and I don't know anyone that would willingly end up here in your position. Maybe this *is* all you have left. You're not a cop. I knew that before I ever agreed to bring you in, but I don't know if I completely believe you. I believe that you think you don't have anything left, but that's very different than actually hitting rock bottom." He leaned back and stroked his bare chin. "Although watching your wife's murder might bring a man pretty close."

A minute passed without anyone saying anything. Joe didn't know what to say. He wasn't going to sit here and justify the past four years of his life to this man, to try to convince him that there wasn't any other path Joe was willing to take. He didn't know if that's what the man was waiting on, for Joe to give more reasons, more conviction. Joe didn't have it in him.

"I'm asking, because, if you haven't hit rock bottom, there's no sense in going forward with this. You have to be willing to die, friend, and if you're not, I don't have much use for you."

Joe still said nothing and the fat man looked at him, staring directly into his eyes without blinking. He stood up, gun in his hand, and walked the three feet to Joe with a surprising quickness, placing the gun against Joe's forehead.

"You're ten seconds from dying. What are your thoughts? One...two...three..."

Joe closed his eyes, listening to the numbers count higher.

"I miss my wife," he said.

"Four..."

"I know I won't see her again, but I miss her."

"Five..."

"I wish I had known my son."

"Six..."

"More than the year he was here, known the person he would become."

"Seven..."

"Eight..."

"I wish I had killed Matthew Brand."

"Nine..."

"That's it."

"Ten..."

Joe felt the gun press down on his head as the fat man pulled the trigger.

Instead of a resounding boom and a single moment of exquisite pain, only a dry click filled the room. The fat man took a step back and put the gun down to his side. Joe opened his eyes, staring at the ground, realizing he was still alive.

"A lot of men piss their pants at that click," Charles said. "You managed to hold your bladder."

Joe didn't look up, his mind nearly blank, besides a numb thought that he had just looked at death.

"I don't know if you're there, but you're close enough. I'll introduce you to Brand; I think you might change your mind about wanting to meet him when you do. That's when we'll see what you know about rock bottom."

* * *

Joe walked down the stairs, his legs not quite sure they could hold him up, grabbing the railing. The house was indeed old, probably built in the sixties or seventies, but last remodeled for sure in the seventies.

"Everyone is out getting dinner right now, but they'll be back soon. You and I should get acquainted first anyway. Take a seat."

Joe looked at the living room, one of those nineteen-nineties big screen TV's sat in the center, turned off. He went to a love seat and sat down. Charles sat in a large chair which seemed to be well built for his oversized body, not creaking in the slightest as he positioned himself on it.

"You and I are worlds apart, and yet, not that far either. Brand killed your dad, your wife, and your son. He killed my brother."

Joe's eyes widened.

"It gets a bit more interesting. My brother's name was Jared Manning, and Brand slit his throat while Jared sat in his patrol car, looking after one of the people they felt sure Brand would come for. Brand came for her, killed my brother, three other cops, and then took her. A lot more news attention was put on the woman than Jared or any of the other cops, but they died the same as everyone else involved. My brother was a cop and I'm a drug dealer. We went down different paths, I guess you could say."

"I'm not looking for the drug trade."

"And you haven't found it. What you've found is a drug dealer who's connected. This right here is my mother's house, or was, and is my house now. The people that are coming back are the people I'm connected to. You're kind of a Godsend, to be honest, Joe. I wasn't sure how we were going to go about doing this before, but now that you're here, we may be able to get some work done."

"What are you talking about and where's my cocaine?"

Charles reached into his pocket, taking him a few seconds because of how tightly strained his pants were against his large legs, and then tossed him the bag. "That's the last one you're getting, so you need to take it slow if you want it to last. When that's done, you're done."

Joe was pulling the table closer to his love seat so that he could break out a line. "What?" He said, pausing.

"You're not going to find Brand, especially this way, with a cocaine addiction. You're going in sober or we can go ahead and end this right here. And by end it here, I don't mean we go our separate ways, I mean I pull the trigger but with one in the chamber this time."

Joe kept his eyes on Charles for a few seconds, then dropped them and finished pulling the table to him.

"I put some of my stuff in there to give it more of a kick. It's better than your bag, so at least you'll go out with a pretty decent high."

"You're not making much sense. In fact, the only thing I'm really understanding is that you'll kill me if I do anything you don't like. I'm getting that pretty clear."

"Take your line and listen."

* * *

Joe lay in a hard bed, feeling like he might just want to get onto the floor and disperse with the notion that he had a mattress at all.

His mind was in a very, very different state.

He normally flew through two different mentalities when on cocaine. The first, almost manic thought, euphoria, and the second, like watching sap drip down a tree, moving so slow as to almost not move at all. Right now, he was—somehow—in both mindsets at once. Charles hadn't lied about the cocaine, it was the best that Joe ever tried and now he could barely move because of it. He wondered if he was going to die, perhaps start with a nosebleed followed by his heart stopping while he lay in this strange bed. Charles talked like he knew what was going on, but that could just be a lot of talk. Maybe the dose Joe ingested was too much, even for an experienced user.

It's not heroin.

True, but he'd never felt like this in his life. His brain was so amped, so hyped up that it had almost frozen—like an engine revved too hard. He couldn't move from the bed, couldn't roll over, couldn't do anything but lie there and think.

Not like there was a shortage of things to think about, though. This Charles guy, Charles Manning—

Joe didn't know whether to believe him or not. He still believed Charles would kill him if he thought Joe might do something stupid; and stupid for Charles seemed to mean involving cops or jeopardizing this operation. Joe planned on doing neither of those, so he thought his life was safe in that regard, but could he believe the rest? That this man, this fat, mid-thirties drug dealer was out here looking for Brand? Had somehow stumbled over the same thing as Joe? Ended up in the sex-slave industry because Brand was here?

He didn't stumble. You stumbled. He saw it from miles off and moved in with the stealth of a snake.

Maybe.

Or maybe the man had simply done a lot of research on Joe before he invited him in and he had ulterior motives. There wasn't any way Joe could tell.

It's too late for all that thinking. That thinking should have been done a long time ago, maybe in the hotel room or maybe before that, even. Now you can't get out of this bed to get a glass of water, so leave the heavy thinking to someone that can.

If Joe listened to himself, and the heavy thinking meant questioning the veracity of Charles' claim, then that left him without much to do except trust.

And how hard was it to believe Charles' story? Any harder than to believe Joe's own?

* * *

"How many people know the name Jared Manning? I bet one percent of the people that read Dillan's second book even remember my brother was a cop, killed while doing his duty," Charles had said.

It seemed, to Joe, that Charles had really internalized that piece: his brother mattered. Joe hadn't needed to internalize that for his wife and child—they were his life—but for Charles, he wanted the world to know that his brother was a person with hopes, aspirations, demons. His brother wasn't a prop.

Charles wasn't a fan of Jeffrey Dillan. Much of the world wasn't either, once the truth came out, although they went ahead and gobbled up the man's book like it was a Thanksgiving turkey. Charles didn't like him because he was a shitty person, and that said something coming from a drug dealer, but Charles also didn't like him because Dillan's book *only* focused on Brand. Everything, in both books, took the viewpoint that Matthew Brand was the only person in the universe who mattered, and the rest of the people on Earth were props to be moved around. Props. That's what his brother, Jared, ended up being to the world, just a prop. Someone that Matthew killed in order to get to the next prop, and that bothered Charles a lot. It made him sick to his stomach when he really started to think about it, which he rarely did anymore. He avoided the subject much like Joe, sans the cocaine. But, still, his brother was a not a fucking prop. That was the point: what the world forgot when they condemned Jeffrey Dillan for basically aiding a serial killer. They forgot it when they read his book. They forgot that the people Brand came into contact with had lives, had families, had an importance outside of their brief interactions with that raving lunatic.

Although, vengeance was an important part of this as well, it seemed to run neck and neck with letting people, or maybe just Charles, know that his brother still mattered. That his life mattered on its own merits.

"We didn't talk much. I don't guess that's a surprise, given my occupation and his."

The whole thing was a surprise. The fact that Charles Manning existed and was walking around in this house swinging a gun and talking about murder was a surprise. The drug dealer/cop brother relationship only added to it.

They didn't talk much, according to Charles, but not because Jared judged him too harshly.

"He knew what I did and he didn't like it. He wasn't one of those law code thumping cops, the kind that would throw you in a gas chamber if the law said it needed to happen. He didn't like what I did because he saw the end effects of it. Kids without parents. Break-ins. Death. The stuff we've been taught drugs lead to since we were old enough to read the DARE signs in school. I don't blame him for that belief, it went with his line of work, and really, I don't blame him for not talking to me anymore. You get over a lot of past grievances pretty quick once someone has died, but I'm sure you understand that as well as anyone, huh?"

They grew apart because Charles wanted to sell drugs while

Jared wanted to serve and protect. Jared married and Charles didn't. Jared had a kid and Charles didn't. The kid was six years old now living with his mother. Charles stopped by when he could, which sounded, to Joe, like a few times each year.

"How long before he died did you talk to him last?"

"I don't know. A year maybe. Saw him at mom's on Christmas, but we didn't say much."

Charles didn't talk about that, about the fact that he didn't exist in his brother's life, and Joe imagined it was for similar reasons as to why he didn't talk about his son's life. What could he really even say about the first year of his son's life? He smiled? He slept? He made messes? And the fact that Joe barely knew his own kid because the child never had the chance to develop created a sadness that he would probably never be able to deal with.

"I looked for Brand after I heard about him breaking out of The Wall that second time. I mean, I didn't look, but I put feelers out. I kept people aware in my circle, kept them looking for a black dude, which brought up a lot of false positives in my line of work." Charles laughed at that. Joe didn't. "It wasn't until this past year that I heard something though. Nothing solid, just birds whistling in trees. I hadn't focused on Brand in a long time, man. I had my business to run and people under me, people close to me, had caught some cases—so I was trying to separate myself from them. Shit was busy, you could say."

The whistling in the trees got his attention though, brought him away from his drug business and even away from the court cases.

He had come east to find Brand.

Charles received a picture from one of his feelers. He wasn't some street dope dealer who people hit up on their phones when they needed a dime bag. He was middle management, connected to the big men and two steps removed from the street hustlers. His feelers could reach a long way, he said, stretching the boundaries of the Midwest. Somehow a picture of a strange looking black dude found its way to Charles' hands. A black guy with blue eyes. A black dude whose past mug shot said he used to have brown eyes. A black dude that had about a million newspaper articles written on him twenty years ago as the first inmate in The Wall. A black dude whose name was Arthur Morgant.

"He was looking for sex slaves. Weirdest shit I've ever seen, man. Here is this guy, wanted by every law enforcement agency in the United States, and he's going through the channels to find himself sex slaves. I didn't understand it at all. And, apparently, he had the people selling fooled, as in they thought he was some guy named Jamal Something-or-Other. I read up on the Morgant character, saw he was a serial rapist, and thought maybe it wasn't Brand at all. Except I kept going back to those blue eyes in that one picture. Then I read about a million times what that doctor in charge of The Wall said. Basically, it was highly probable that Matthew Brand had implanted his own brain over Morgant's. So, I thought, fuck it."

Morgant was going to die; whether Morgant turned out to be a rapist or a cop killer, the man was going to die.

Charles used everything, every bit of muscle, of political capital, of connections he had, to work his way into the sex trade. He made the transition and now he was simply a delivery man. He'd left middle-management for a job on the road and he didn't regret it at all. Because it was going to, at some point, put him in contact with Matthew Brand.

"I mean, once that letter came out, it all made sense. He's

198

using these Asians for the bodies that he's going to blow up the Earth with, or whatever he plans on doing. I don't really care about all that. I just want to be able to make one delivery to him, face to face, and that will be the end of him. He isn't going to get the chance to blow anyone up."

When Charles heard about some guy wanting to know more from Sally, who despite what she told Joe, sold women off left and right (which was how she knew Charles), he got Joe Welch's name. From there, he looked up just about everything he could find on the man in the hotel room who was all of a sudden interested in sex slaves.

"And then, well, I thought it would be a good idea for us to meet. If it didn't work out, you wouldn't be the first guy I've had to kill because things didn't work out."

* * *

There was a plan to all this. One that would go into effect fairly shortly, although Charles didn't list out a timeline.

Joe had to be sober. That's one thing he understood, one thing that Charles made extremely clear.

"I can't have any coke head running around fucking with my plan. I'm not going to trust this to some drug."

So Joe lay in bed, higher than any kite could ever hope to rise, understanding intellectually that this was the last time he would be high. He would either sober up or die, Charles told him. Joe had no idea what that *really* meant, only that sobering up could have some serious physical side effects. He didn't know which ones and really wasn't in much of a state to think about them.

The plan. That's what he cared about. Charles' plan.

And it was quite simple, quite terrifying, and quite beautiful.

Joe was going to turn into a sex slave and Charles was going to drop him off for Brand. And then, they would kill him.

20

Twenty

"Say it again. So that we both can understand you," Art said into the conference call.

"We could use him. I talked to his parents already, and they said, you know, if we could guarantee the guy's safety then they would let us talk to him about it," Gyle answered.

"You think he'll talk to *us*?" Jake asked.

"Yeah, I do. I mean, if he knows how much he could help us, I really think he would."

"And Brand doesn't know?" Jake asked.

"Fuck no," Art said. "I didn't even know until this phone call. You think if he knew he'd be out there trying to blow up the sun? What are you going to do, Gyle?"

The recording only played silence for the next few seconds as Matthew listened.

"I'm going to call him. He's young, still in high school and he never met Brand, or Rally either for that matter. Still, he could help us if Brand spoke with him."

"What's he going to say to Brand? What could he possibly say?" Jake asked.

"I imagine something along the lines of, 'Hey, I'm your son.'"

* * *

Matthew played the recording back and listened to it ten times. It was only five minutes long, but he studied each word with complete concentration. He listened to each syllable with all the brain cells he could muster together, paying closer attention than he had in any college classroom.

A son.

That's what they were talking about.

That Matthew Brand had a son out there. Not Hilman. This boy's name, and that's what he was at seventeen years old, was Vick. Short for Victor, Matthew imagined. Rally had known. It must have been at the end of their marriage, around the time that Matthew figured out how he could bring Hilman back, finally worked out all the equations. Rally said she was leaving then, said that she wouldn't stay married to a mad-man, and he had let her go. Had she been pregnant? It was possible. They never stopped making love. Even in their thirties they acted like they were in their early twenties, finding times to go at each other even when there appeared to be no time. Yes, it was possible. And would she have told him?

No. I wouldn't have. You already know the answer to that, Rally said.

Matthew didn't chase the intrusion of her voice away. Maybe he didn't even recognize it as an intrusion, but the closest thing he could find to actually asking Rally herself whether or not they had a second child.

I wouldn't have told you anything about a baby because you had already lost your mind at that point. There would be no telling what you would have done. Brainwashed him into helping you as he grew older? Used him as a battery for Hilman's life, the same as you did the police?

Never, Matthew answered.

How would I have known? All I knew was that you were going out into the world to kill cops and I wouldn't let you have anything to do with a newborn baby.

What about an abortion? Matthew asked.

You know how I felt about that.

He did. For all the women's rights and liberal thoughts that Rally espoused, abortion was not one of them. The child had a right to life, and no one could take that right away, according to her.

So, what, you gave it up? Gave it away to an adoption agency?

What else would I have done? Kept the thing? Kept it around me so that you could find out within a few months of me finally showing and then back to Crazy Town I went? No, Matt.

She was right. Rally would have had the kid secretly, quite possibly letting the FBI or some other police agency know for tracking purposes, and then given the child away.

And now, this kid, this man, was trying to get in contact with his father? Was trying to find Matthew?

What do I do? Matthew asked Rally, asked the voice in his head.

What do you want to do? The voice asked back.

I want to find my son.

To be continued in Book Three: The Devil's Dream: Waking Up. Grab your copy now!

On Purpose and Other Things

Thanks for reading, and I mean that wholeheartedly. I love telling stories and without you, that wouldn't be possible.

I know at the end of books, a lot of writers offer you something free if you sign-up for their mailing list. What they're doing, essentially, is buying your email address.

I don't want to do that.

I think having a purpose in life is important. It adds clarity and meaning to what you do. I'm lucky to know mine and that purpose dictates my life: I'm here to tell stories. Nothing else even comes close to the happiness this job gives me.

With that said, if you like reading my novels and want to know when the next book comes out, sign-up below. No tricks. No buying your address. Just me telling stories and you enjoying them.

The way these relationships should work.

Join here: http://www.davidbeersfiction.com/splashpageic2

The Devil's Dream: Part III

Chapter One

Matthew parked his van in the middle of the road. He opened the door and stepped out, not bothering to look behind him. There wasn't anything to look at back there that he couldn't see in front of him. He closed the door of his van and stood alone on Boylston Street in downtown Boston. It was noon, and on any day during the past fifty years, Boylston Street would have been busy. It would have been packed with people walking up and down the sidewalks, with cars waiting in traffic, perhaps honking, perhaps only idling. Shops would have been open with people entering and exiting at an almost constant rate. Hot or cold, rain or shine, Boylston Street would have been busy.

Not now, though.

Now, Boylston Street, for lack of a better term, was dead.

The blood cells of the street no longer flowed; a few cars were parallel parked, but the vast majority, the cars that filled the roads day in and day out, were gone. Where to? Probably driven to family members, to friends, all in other states. South, most likely, because nothing north would be any different than this. No cars sat at stop lights, none made rights or lefts, no taxis available to pick up pedestrians. The streets were devoid of the machinery that had filled them since Henry Ford's time.

Matthew turned around slowly, taking in everything around him. Had he done this? Had he really taken an entire city and moved it?

The people that should have populated the sidewalks and the businesses were missing as well, gone with the cars. The sidewalks were empty of life, holding only shards of broken glass from the looted shops above them. Matthew looked up toward the window of an electronics store, a huge window that had once stretched across the entire second story, showing all of the merchandise for sale. Now, there was no window, only a hole in the side of the building, and whatever merchandise once glittered in the sunlight was gone. Directly below the store sat the remnants of a television, though difficult to tell as the pieces were scattered across the pavement. Someone had accidentally pushed it off the ledge in their attempt to steal it, though in this city, how did they plan to plug it in? Not a single outlet anywhere in Boston worked, anywhere in Massachusetts for that matter. Maybe this final resting place was the appropriate spot for the television because nothing in Boston would ever 'work' again. No televisions, no computers, no light bulbs, no nothing. Matthew imagined that if he walked into a few of these empty stores, he would end up finding someone: the homeless, the mentally deranged, the people that had literally nowhere else in the world they could go. If given enough time though, Matthew imagined they too would leave the city. That or die off. There was nothing here for them either, now that they couldn't panhandle any longer. No money to be given out and nothing left to be taken. Unfortunately, none of those people would have the time to migrate somewhere else. In two weeks, everything would be in darkness. Boston. New York. London. Antarctica.

Maybe not. You don't have to make that decision yet, not until you've met him. Then you can make it. You need to meet him though;

206

you need to see if he's your son, if he's our son.

Rally again. No invitation necessary anymore; those days were long past. No, she came and went as she pleased, giving her thoughts and listening to his. She was right though, even if he didn't want to admit it. Matthew wasn't going to pull the trigger if his son was out there, not until they met. Then, maybe he would and maybe he wouldn't, but there was a lot to think about. The FBI knew of this kid, his son, and if they somehow tried to connect the two of them, it was only to apprehend Matthew. They wouldn't let Matthew meet his blood and then go on his merry way. No, if they met, and the FBI knew about it, Brand was as good as dead, most likely through a new hole in the side of his head.

There'll be time for that later, he told the voice in his head. He wasn't sure if he was talking to himself or to Rally anymore. Not the actual Rally, not the one in the ground, but the only one that still lived. Just as he had copied himself into Morgant, maybe he had copied Rally into himself, so maybe she *was* talking to him. Or maybe his brain was continuing to shutdown and her voice only the sparks of misfiring synapses. He was finding, more and more, that he didn't care either way. He wasn't trying to block her out, wasn't trying to deny her—he appreciated the conversations because he knew they would be the last he ever had with anyone.

Matthew came to Boston to see his accomplishments. He could read about them online or hear about them on the news, but he had wanted to witness it himself. His goal was to throw the world into darkness, and here he had a small glimpse of what that might look like. The sun still shown from above, but inside the buildings surrounding him, blackness lived. There was only death and a world coming undone. Matthew would see about his son and then see about ending the world.

#

Joe Welch's whole body shivered. Not once, not like a chill had overcome him, but constantly. His stomach muscles flexed and released so many times that they had finally cramped an hour ago. Now he was curled up on his bed, unable to straighten his body because of the cramping; goosebumps and sweat covered his skin. A blanket lay over him, but still he shivered. Constant shivering.

His body was dirty. Piss covered his sheets. Most of the time he could make it to the bathroom for the diarrhea, but not always. A pile of sheets lay in the corner, covered in shit; he shoved them off his bed during one of the moments when he could actually move. This wasn't one of those moments, however. Really, he couldn't remember the last time he had been able to straighten up, to walk, to move. He pissed himself at will now, not caring about the smell or how the urine felt when it finally cooled on his leg.

He didn't know how many days he'd been in this room, shivering and soiling himself. Three? Twenty? He knew that someone came in from time to time with water and food, but that was all. They didn't make any effort to help him, to clean him, to do anything besides provide the bare essentials. The light in the ceiling remained on, even at night. Joe didn't care. He barely noticed. His world was dark, so dark, and his body wrecked with pain. Electric shocks came in waves, starting in his hands and feet and moving up through his appendages. Headaches tore through his thoughts, rendering him unable to recognize the people dropping off food and water. Sometimes he scurried over on hands and knees, like a rat, and downed the water—only to throw it back up all over the white bread sandwich sitting on the tray beneath him. Nothing stayed down, and the stuff that came out, no matter what hole, was little more than water.

Sometimes when the fever faded for a minute, Joe would think. Or, at least, he would try to think. Why was he here? Why was this happening? And he could remember if he tried hard. This was years of cocaine leaving his body. This was his central nervous system, which had grown dependent on the white substance, realizing there was no more. This was a fever wracking his brain because he denied his body a substance it demanded, a substance that someone downstairs said he couldn't have anymore. AND WHY WHY WHY WHY COULD HE NOT HAVE IT?

Patricia. Jason.

Those two names floated through sometimes, when his body relented for a second from its seemingly eternal agony. He would remember those two people, the beautiful woman he lay with and the young son he fathered. It was for them, the reason he couldn't have any more powder. Not because the man downstairs with the gun said he couldn't, but because if he used anymore, the man downstairs would kill him. Which, on its own was fine, but he hadn't come to this old house and been locked in this room to die. He had come because all he wanted in this life was to avenge those names. So if he didn't go through this, if he didn't face this pain and dirt, then his death meant no vengeance.

Sometimes he could focus on that, but most of the time, he shook and shivered on the bed, his body out of his control and his mind boiling with fever.

#

"He's heard you?" Gyle asked.

"He had to. He's heard everything Jake said over the past few weeks, and there's no reason to think he would have missed this one."

"But he hasn't contacted you about it?"

"No, but that doesn't mean anything either. He knows what we said, without a doubt, we just need to make sure he believes us."

Art, Jake, and Gyle sat at a large conference table, meant for twelve people rather than the three currently using it. A large, flat screen television hung on the wall, showing a picture of a young, white male.

"I know you guys want to continue going through these photos, but I'm not even certain this is the right path to take," Gyle said. "I don't want to send someone at Brand only to have that someone end up dead. This has to work. Brand has to believe us and right now, we don't have any indication that he does."

Jake leaned his elbows onto the table, turning his chair away from the television screen and to Gyle at the other end of the room. "What's the best way to make him believe us? Have his kid call him. If he talks to someone he thinks is his offspring, it's going to trigger a whole host of emotions. Think about it, Gyle. A large portion of Brand's adult life has been an attempt to reclaim his family. We're presenting him with a piece of family that he didn't even know existed. It could change everything about this, just one phone call. We don't have to make the guy operative; we just need a phone call to test the waters. From there, we can figure the rest out."

Gyle sighed and leaned back in his chair. "Fine. Who's this guy?" He motioned to the television.

"His name is Henry Werzen," Art said. "He's twenty-four

years old and this is his first year with the FBI. He has his law degree from Duke, but never took the bar, instead simply applied to us."

"Where's he live?" Gyle asked.

"He's currently in southern California. He lives with his brother who is twenty-two and finishing up college. Werzen's smart. Graduated top five in his law class and apparently got a perfect score on his SAT."

"More," Jake said, "he could pass for eighteen years old. We've mapped out the time line, and if Brand conceived a child five years into his original search to bring Hilman back, right now the kid would be eighteen. So we need someone that looks young."

Art turned to the picture on the screen. The kid did appear young, much younger than Jake. He wore glasses and his hair was tossed over to the side, messy like. He could pass for eighteen, easy.

"Have you talked to him?" Gyle asked.

"No. We haven't reached out to any of these potentials yet. We wanted to vet them by you first, but we think he might be our best shot," Art answered.

"Why?"

"He's smart. He's not married. And reading up on him, it seems like he's a goddamn patriot. Kid goes to law school with the only intention of signing up to work with the FBI after. He's put two cases in the black during his first year, so he's working hard. Plus, he looks the part. Look at his face; he looks like a nerd, just like Brand at the same age. Same color blue eyes too, which is huge. Brand sees those, the psycho is going to melt."

Art watched Gyle nod, seeming to take it all in. "Alright, if we put him on this, do you guys have a plan lined up?"

Jake smiled. "Yeah, kind of."

"What is it?"

"You sure you want to hear this, Gyle?" Art asked. "If you ask what we're about to do, there goes plausible deniability."

Art looked on as Gyle's eyes bore down onto him. His face was stoic, his lips set. Art could tell him their plan and the whole thing might be shut down, because really, the plan wasn't something a rocket scientist would create during his down time. The plan involved a great deal of risk, a great deal of luck, and it involved this young kid—Henry—playing his part perfectly. It also meant that the kid could end up dead pretty quick, with Jake and Art standing around holding their dicks. If Gyle knew about this and shit went bad, then he would be standing there with them, all three jerking off in front of the nation.

"Fuck you, Art. Yeah, I want to know. This isn't politics anymore and we're about to send a kid fresh off his mom's tit to deal with Brand. I want to know what you and the boy genius over here have cooked up."

"Alright, boss. Your choice."

Art told him the plan.

To be continued in Book Three:
The Devil's Dream: Waking Up

Also by David Beers

Nemesis

She's coming and no one can stop her...

An alien Queen, Morena, was removed from power and forced into exile. Doomed to roam space forever, with no hope of return.

Until a random party brings a man named Michael to her crashed ship. For the first time in millennia, Morena sees her salvation. First, in Michael ... and then Earth. The perfect place to repopulate her species. And those already here? **They can bow or die.**

As Morena begins her conquest, can Michael warn the world before it's too late? Can anyone stop the most powerful force the world has ever seen?

Earth's final Nemesis has arrived.

Don't miss this pulse-pounding science fiction series! If you love thought provoking thrill-rides, grab this book today!
* * *
The Singularity

One thousand years in the future, humans no longer rule...

In the early twenty-first century, humanity marveled at its greatest creation: Artificial Intelligence. They never foresaw the consequences of such a creation, though...

Now, in a world where humans must meet specifications to continue living, a man named Caesar emerges. Different, both in thought and talent, Caesar somehow slipped through the genetic net meant to catch those like him.

Eyes are falling on Caesar now, though, and he can no longer hide. The Artificial Intelligence wants him dead, but others want him to lead their revolution...

Can one man stand against humanity's greatest creation?
A don't-miss epic science fiction novel that pits one man fighting for the future of all people!
* * *

Red Rain

What would you do if you couldn't stop killing?

John Hilt lives The American Dream. His corner office looks out on Dallas's beautiful skyline. His amazing wife and children love him. His father and sister adore him. John has it all.

Except every few years, when Harry shows back up. Harry wants John to kill people. Harry wants to watch the world burn.

Murderous thoughts take hold of John, and as flames ignite

across his life, the sky doesn't send cool rain water, but blood to feed their hunger.

If you love taut, psychological thrillers, grab Red Rain today and prepare to sleep with the lights on!

* * *

The Devil's Dream

He'll raise the dead, at all costs...

Perhaps the smartest man to ever live, Matthew Brand changed the world by twenty-five years old. In his mid-thirties, he still shaped the world as he wanted, until cops gunned down his son on the street.

Brand's life changed then. He forgot about bettering Earth and started trying to resurrect his son.

Eventually, Brand's mind overpowered even death's mysteries; he discovered how to bring back the dead--he only needed living bodies to make his son's life possible again. Why not use the bodies of those who killed his son?

In the largest manhunt the FBI's ever experienced, how do they stop a man who can calculate all the odds and stack them in his favor?